ANY MAN CAN BE COMPLETELY TRAINED IN 7 DAYS— THE LOVEHOUSE WAY!

For the first time in print, here is Dr. Barbara Lovehouse's famous method for making *every* man a good man. Barbara Lovehouse knows there are no bad men—only *inexperienced* women: women who simply need to learn the proven techniques Dr. Lovehouse has developed in over fifty years of training *every* type of man.

Now you can turn moody men, disagreeable men, roving men, and disobedient men into loving companions eager to fetch (furs, flowers, engagement rings), to please (in and out of bed), and to remain faithful (at parties, in bars, even when meeting old girlfriends). And just as you've seen Barbara demonstrate on her national TV appearances, you can teach your man to stop cringing when he hears such words as "jacket and tie," "commitment," "marriage," and "pregnant."

NO BAD MEN includes the complete Lovehouse Training Philosophy: the key words that set off a joyous response, such as "how *huuuge*" . . . valuable tips for getting that "tail" up! . . . and a foolproof test to help you choose the right breed of man for you. Yes, Dr. Barbara Lovehouse gives you all you need to develop a man's natural instincts to love, honor, and obey—without the use of the choke chain! Remember, with the Lovehouse Way, there really are—

NO BAD MEN

No Bad Men

Training Your Man the Lovehouse Way

by Dr. Barbara Lovehouse
as told to Anna Sequoia
and Sarah Gallick

Illustrations by
Susan Bissett

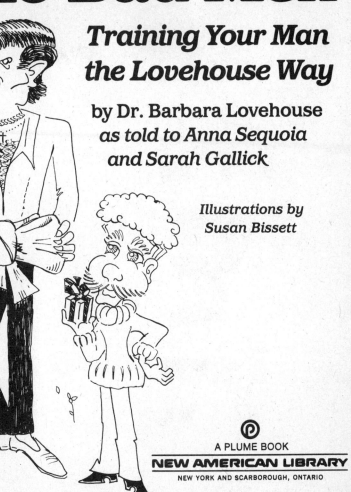

A PLUME BOOK

NEW AMERICAN LIBRARY

NEW YORK AND SCARBOROUGH, ONTARIO

NAL BOOKS ARE AVAILABLE AT QUANTITY DISCOUNTS WHEN USED TO
PROMOTE PRODUCTS OR SERVICES. FOR INFORMATION PLEASE WRITE
TO PREMIUM MARKETING DIVISION, NEW AMERICAN LIBRARY,
1633 BROADWAY, NEW YORK, NEW YORK 10019.

Interior photographs by Anna Sequoia, Debra Siegel,
Marlene Siegel Rosenberg, and Robert Siegel

PLUME TRADEMARK REG. U.S. PAT. OFF. AND FOREIGN COUNTRIES
REGISTERED TRADEMARK—MARCA REGISTRADA
HECHO EN HARRISONBURG, VA., U.S.A.

SIGNET, SIGNET CLASSIC, MENTOR, PLUME, MERIDIAN and NAL BOOKS
are published *in the United States* by New American Library, 1633 Broadway,
New York, New York 10019, *in Canada* by The New American Library of
Canada Limited, 81 Mack Avenue, Scarborough, Ontario M1L 1M8

LIBRARY OF CONGRESS CATALOGING IN PUBLICATION DATA

Lovehouse, Barbara.
  No bad men.
  1. Men—Anecdotes, facetiae, satire, etc. I. Sequoia,
Anna. II. Gallick, Sarah. III. Title.
PN6231.M45L6 1984 818'.5402   84-2080
ISBN 0-452-25502-3

Designed by Sharen DuGoff Egana

First Printing, June, 1984

1 2 3 4 5 6 7 8 9

PRINTED IN THE UNITED STATES OF AMERICA

She who accepts fake jewels
must also fake orgasms.

—Barbara Lovehouse

Acknowledgments

I would like to acknowledge the cooperation and support of the following people: Richard Gruber, Dot and Richard Hildreth, Norbert Katz, Carol Kramer, Joe Kramer, Nancy McCarthy, John Paulsen, Marlene Siegel-Rosenberg, Ira Rosenberg, Hal and Judy Schneider, Bushey and Peggy Schneider, Debra Siegel, Robert Siegel, Richard Tworek, and Natasha Wilson. Also, thanks to my editor, Claudia Reilly, and a very special thank you to Diane Cleaver, my agent.

Anna Sequoia

I'd like to thank Barbara Woodhouse, Barbara Cartland, and each of those who helped with this book. You know who you are.

Sarah Gallick

Table of Contents

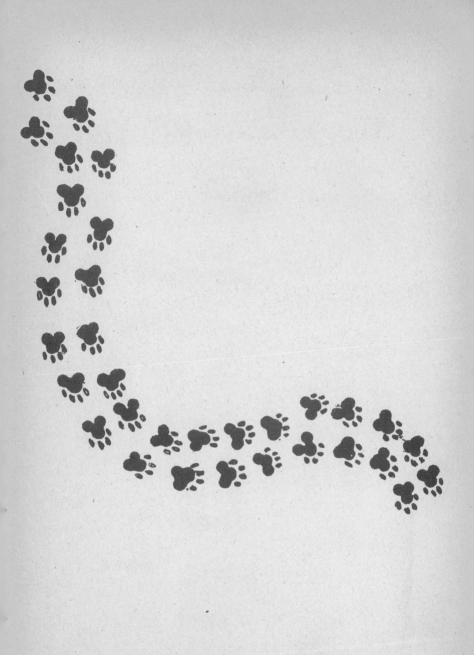

INTRODUCTION

Real Men *Can* Be Good

Not only can real men be good, they can be *real* good.

Rhett Butler was good to Scarlett O'Hara.
John Lennon was good to Yoko Ono.
Even Onassis was good to Jackie O.
So why isn't your man good to you?

The sad truth is that most men, unlike women, lack proper training. Think back to your childhood. You were trained to be generous, thoughtful, honest, gentle, and clean. Meanwhile, the little boy down the street was trained to be a man. And what does it mean *to be a man?* It means *to stand up when you urinate.*

I, Dr. Barbara Lovehouse, intend to change this sorry state of affairs. It is my contention that *any* man can be trained to be good.

- *Your* man can clean the hair out of the tub!
- *Your* man can cook beef stroganoff!
- *Your* man can even get down on his knees and propose!

Seventy-five years ago, I opened my first training school for dogs. So successful was my work that I soon had women begging me to let their men enroll in my course. Foolishly, I bowed to these ladies' wishes. Within a week their men were more manageable. Unfortunately, their men were also walking on all fours and eating Alpo out of bowls. I quickly ejected the men from the classroom.

Since those early days of experimentation, I have progressed considerably in my ability to train men,

and can assure you that the side effects of training are no more dangerous for men than the Pill is for women.

I have never met a bad man—only a poorly trained one. And, although you may not be able to teach an old dog new tricks, you can properly train a man of any age. The important thing is to begin training immediately after you meet him, before he has a chance to exhibit his bad habits. Your man will be good if shown the correct way to behave.

Now you may ask, hasn't he had any training before? The answer is simple: No. If any woman in his past had ever bothered to train him, he would never have strayed from her side. A trained man is a faithful man.

There are many women who insist men don't require training. They believe that by showing a man love and giving him everything he wants, he will reciprocate with equal love and generosity. They are, of course, totally wrong. Think of your poor mother and how miserably that approach worked for *her.*

Of course, training a man requires some sophistication. It would be nice if things could be settled with a rolled-up newspaper, but alas, it's rarely that easy. Most men (and for that matter, most dogs) respond better to words than to whips.

Men, like dogs, thrive on affection and praise. No man can be told too often that he is handsome, brilliant, and sexy. Screaming at a man is effective only on rare occasions.

Here I am with the first man I trained. He was quite splendid
at retrieving bones, but rather vulgar at dinner parties . . .

. . . Here I am with the same man after perfecting
my training techniques. As you can see, I have learned
the subtle differences between dogs and men.

Now, if you can't beat them and you can't scream at them, you may wonder what you *can* do with them. *Say what you mean and mean what you say.* The little schnauzer who chews up your slippers is never going to break the habit as long as he senses you will accept his behavior. By the same token, a man who's been led to believe it was perfectly all right to show up at your apartment last Saturday night with a six-pack of beer and a *TV Guide* is not going to show up at your door *this* Saturday night with champagne and theater tickets.

When should you begin to train your man? I prefer to start training at six months of age. But let's say your man is slightly older. Can a 20-year-old be trained to put down the toilet seat? Yes. Can a 30-year-old learn to propose? Certainly. Can a 40-year-old be taught to be cordial to his mother-in-law? Most definitely! Even an 80-year-old man can be immeasurably improved by a few weeks of training. With determination you can prove it's never too late. Remember, he may be 6 feet 2 inches, with a beard and a past, but underneath, he's still a puppy in search of a fire hydrant.

CHAPTER 1

Does *Your* Man Need Training?

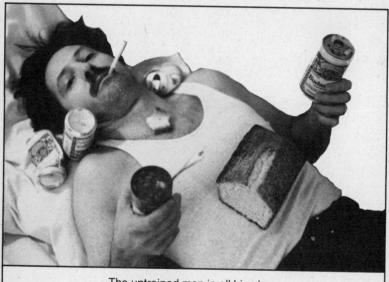

The untrained man in all his glory.

The best way to determine whether your man needs training is to examine certain items found in your home. The first item to examine is your man's wallet. The next time your man is snoring on your couch, carefully remove his wallet from his pants and spread its contents on a table. Now compare the contents of your man's wallet with the contents shown in the photographs opposite. Do the items in your man's wallet bear resemblance to Exhibit A or Exhibit B?

| Exhibit A | Exhibit B |

Another item you should examine in order to determine whether your man needs training is your face.

Go take a peek in a mirror. Does your face resemble the one in Exhibit A or the one in Exhibit B?

| Exhibit A | Exhibit B |

Two additional items you must examine in order to discover whether your man needs training are your hands. Look down. Are your hands like the ones in Exhibit A or Exhibit B?

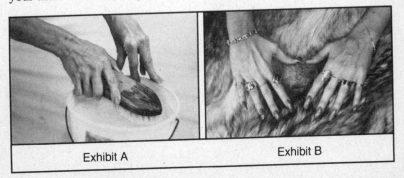

| Exhibit A | Exhibit B |

If you consistently picked Exhibit A for your answer, your man probably needs training. But just to be certain, look at the following chart and see which tricks your man can perform.

Five Tricks the Untrained Man Knows	**Five Tricks the Trained Man Knows**
1. Play dead	1. Fetch (fur coats, not bones)
2. Beg	2. Jump (when you snap your fingers)
3. Roll over	3. Up pretty (in bed)
4. Lay down	4. Speak (to your mother)
5. Come	5. Stay (with you)

Still not convinced your man needs training? Ask yourself the following series of questions. For every "Yes" answer, give your man the points indicated, then turn to the end of the quiz to see how he rates.

QUIZ

1. Does your man expect you to do things for him?   (5 points)
   Like cook his dinner?   (10 points)
   And brush his teeth?   (20 points)

2. Could your man's appearance be improved?   (5 points)
   By purchasing a nice suit?   (5 points)
   Made of armor?   (10 points)

3. Does your man like to sleep?   (0 points)
   In the nude?   (0 points)
   With his buddy?   (20 points)

4. Do you ever get angry with your man?   (5 points)
   For making messes?   (10 points)
   In his pants?   (20 points)

Does your man ever get on your nerves?

5. Could your love life be improved?   (5 points)
   By doing something different?   (5 points)
   Like having sex?   (20 points)

6. Does your man like to go exploring?   (0 points)
   In new and exciting places?   (0 points)
   Such as your wallet?   (10 points)

7. Do you ever daydream about your man?   (0 points)
   Being murdered?   (10 points)
   By you?   (20 points)

8. Has your man ever forgotten your birthday?   (5 points)
   Your anniversary?   (5 points)
   Your name?   (10 points)

9. Does your man ever get on your nerves?   (5 points)
   When he does stupid little things?   (5 points)
   Like breathe?   (10 points)

10. Does your man get along with your girlfriends?   (0 points)
    Real well?   (5 points)
    In bed?   (20 points)

Scoring:
0 points—You lied.
5 points or more—You are stuck with an untrained man. Read on . . .

"If you pick up a starving dog and make him prosperous, he will not bite you. This is the principal difference between a dog and a man."

—MARK TWAIN

CHAPTER 2

Men vs. Dogs: Some Clear-cut Comparisons

"YOU HEEL!"

I have worked with men and I have worked with dogs, and I've come to the following conclusion: Dogs are easier to train. While we're on the subject, I might also point out that dogs are generally cuter than men. Yes, it's true that the average man won't piddle on your rug, but then the average dog won't leave you for a younger woman.

Before you rush out to get yourself a man, consider the dog: affectionate, fluffy, loyal, trustworthy. Still not convinced? Then use this comparison table.

What Can a Man Do That a Dog Can't Do Better?

Commands:	The Dog	The Man
Sit Up pretty	Yes	Prefers to slouch
Speak	Yes	Not when you want him to
Fetch	Yes	Prefers to make *you* fetch
Roll over	Yes	Only to steal the covers
Play dead	Yes	Yes—especially in bed
Come	Yes	Yes—especially in someone else's bed
Stay	Yes	Only when you are trying to make him go away
Wag-a-tail	Yes	No—it will break
Heel	Yes	Not even when proposing

Both men and dogs, however, do have certain vexsome little problems in common. To assist my gentle reader in comparing their relative virtues (or lack thereof), I have compiled the following list:

Male Dogs' Problems vs.	Men's Problems
Dogs jump on people.	Men jump on people, too, especially on attractive women.
Dogs bark.	Men tell sexist jokes.
Dogs chew on shoes and furniture.	Men chew disgusting cigars.
Dogs dig holes in backyards.	Men dig holes in your bank account.
Dogs wet on rugs.	Men put wet glasses down on wood furniture.
Dogs have strong odors.	Men have strong odors, too.
Dogs get fleas and ticks.	Men get herpes and other venereal diseases.
Dogs run out of the house.	Men run around.
Dogs urinate on fence posts.	Men urinate on toilet seats.
Dogs nip people.	Men nip booze.
Dogs shed.	Men lose their hair.
Dogs are mean to cats.	Men are mean to women.
Dogs never wash their own dishes.	Men never wash their own dishes either.
Dogs whine.	Men complain, criticize, *and* whine.
Dogs bite.	Men hit.
Dogs don't brush their teeth before they have sex.	Men don't either.
Dogs are constantly horny.	Men are only horny when *you* aren't.
Dogs will mount your leg if not castrated.	Men will mount your cousin's leg if not castrated.
Dogs are generally not well-read.	Men aren't either.

FIVE THINGS MEN CAN DO THAT DOGS CAN'T

A dog can't buy you anything but love, whereas the properly trained man can buy you anything.

A dog can't take you out for dinner. You're welcome to join Fido as he munches away at his meal, but you'll probably get a sore back from eating on the floor.

A dog can't make love to you—no matter what the Happy Hooker led you to believe.

A dog can't kiss you neck. While most dogs will lick your neck, it's just not the same thing.

A dog can't wash your kitchen floor. Neither can he wax it.

On the other hand, men do have their uses. You wouldn't want to go to the symphony with a dog, would you? And just imagine the look on your father's face if some mutt came to the door and announced he was going to marry you.

There is one final point to keep in mind when choosing between a man and a dog: Men don't have to be walked on cold winter mornings.

Ladies, the choice is yours.

> *"(Men are) the only animals that have money and buy champagne."*
>
> —MARLENE DIETRICH

CHAPTER 3

To Train or Not to Train: Is This Man a Potential Mate?

Occasionally, a client who is baby-sitting for her neighbor's dog will bring the animal to me for training. I, in turn, will point out to her that it's useless to train a dog that is only going to be in your home for a few days or weeks. Train your *own* dog, and let your neighbor worry about the one that belongs to *her*.

Similarly, I believe it's ridiculous to train a man with whom you don't plan to spend much time. The "quickie" you meet at the office Christmas party doesn't require training. Your husband does.

Men You Should Never Train	*Men You Should Always Train*
Your bus driver	Your boyfriend
Your priest	Your husband
Your state senator	Your father
Your waiter	Your son

A Few Words About Joy Riders

Would you want your mother to meet this man?

When you first meet a man, it is imperative that you decide whether he is a *Potential Mate* or—more likely—a *Joy Rider*. What is a *Potential Mate*? A marriageable man. What is a *Joy Rider*? A lot of fun.

Joy Riders proposition you in elevators.
Potential Mates don't.

Joy Riders wear black leather pants.
Potential Mates don't.

Joy Riders make your girlfriends green with envy.
Potential Mates don't.

Joy Riders make you faint when you kiss.
Potential Mates don't.

Joy Riders look like Robert Redford.
Potential Mates don't.

Joy Riders know where your G Spot is.
Potential Mates don't.

Joy Riders dance until dawn.
Potential Mates don't.

Joy Riders drive Corvettes.
Potential Mates don't.

A Few Words About Potential Mates

Although *Potential Mates* have their dull moments, they do possess one remarkable quality: They are *reliable.*

Potential Mates don't snort coke in your bathroom.
Joy Riders do.

Potential Mates don't laugh off suicide threats.
Joy Riders do.

Potential Mates don't look like the men on the covers of romance novels.
Joy Riders do.

Potential Mates don't give you the bill for their "sister's" abortion.
Joy Riders do.

Potential Mates don't write you letters from prison.
Joy Riders do.

Potential Mates don't borrow your paycheck.
Joy Riders do.

Potential Mates don't flirt with your daughters.
Joy Riders do.

Potential Mates don't have you subpoenaed as their character witness.
Joy Riders do.

When to Take a Joy Ride and When to Train

Why would any sane woman embark on a Joy Ride? Believe it or not, there are three excellent reasons. A woman should take a Joy Ride if:

1. **She is married to an untrained man.**
2. **She is desperate for sex.**
3. **She is in the process of training *another* man to feel jealousy.**

YOU'RE MOST LIKELY TO MEET A
POTENTIAL MATE AT HIS WIFE'S FUNERAL
BUT BEWARE OF COMPETITION.

Let us presume that if you are about to embark on a Joy Ride, it is for one of these reasons.

Now, the woman who is having a Joy Ride must not concern herself with extensive training sessions. Only one rule applies: Keep your relationship short and sweet. A Joy Ride should begin a few minutes after you meet a suitable *Joy Rider*, and it should end within a few months.

But, let us suppose that you have just met a man and you are uncertain as to whether he is a *Joy Rider* or a *Potential Mate*. It is crucial for you to know immediately, because a *Potential Mate* must begin his training course the very second his eyes meet yours. To help you decide, I have prepared the following table.

How to Distinguish the Joy Rider from the Potential Mate

The Joy Rider

The ideal *Joy Rider* is disease-free. Before saying "Hello" to him, watch for a few seconds to see if he scratches any parts of his body. (*Note:* This is not a foolproof test.)

The Potential Mate

The ideal *Potential Mate* is unmarried. Before saying "Hello" to him, watch for a few seconds to see if he wears a wedding band. (*Note:* This is not a foolproof test.)

Where You're Likely to Meet a Joy Rider:

- In the backseat of a car

- At a singles' bar
- In a dark alley

- In the men's bathroom
- On certain Aegean beaches
- In a courtroom (he's the defendant)

Where You're Likely to Meet a Potential Mate:

- At your younger sister's wedding
- In the library of a law school
- In the library of a medical school
- At the White House
- At his wife's funeral
- In a courtroom (he's the judge)

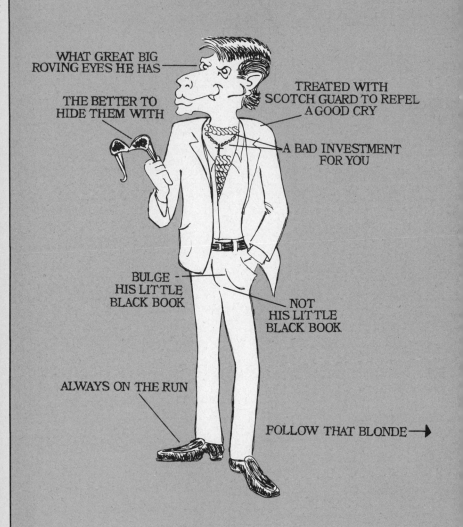

THE POTENTIAL MATE

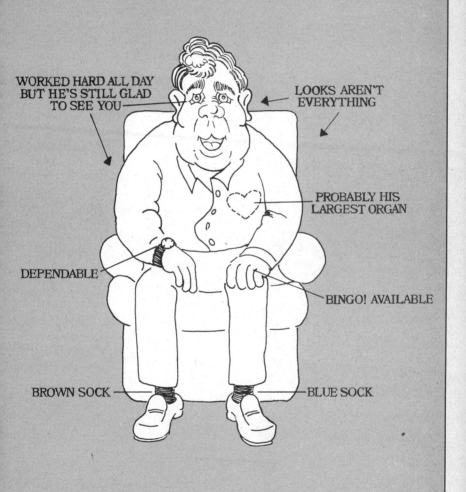

Five Ways to Recognize a Joy Rider:

1. He tells you his name is John Doe.
2. He offers you money after you make love.
3. He *asks* you for money after you make love.
4. He dances well.
5. He wears oil on his hair and chains on his chest.

Five Ways to Recognize a Potential Mate:

1. He lets you go first (and I'm not merely talking about doors).
2. He asks you to his apartment for dinner and actually cooks a meal.
3. He asks you to his mother's house for dinner. (*Note:* If he cooks the meal, marry him that night—he's already trained.)
4. He doesn't dance—or if he does, he shouldn't.
5. He blushes when you compliment him.

One Thing the Joy Rider Always Asks When He Meets You:

"You as horny as I am?"

One Thing the Potential Mate Always Asks When He Meets You:

"What's your name?"

What Joy Riders Say:

"Thanks, babe."

"Thanks a lot, babe."
"See you around, babe."

What Potential Mates Say:

"I have all this money—I just don't know how to spend it."
"You'd look great in a fur coat."
"I'd rather give than receive."

For a happy Joy Ride, do not select a man you must see daily, such as your boss or your father. Do select a frisky, disease-free specimen with clear eyes, healthy gums, and shiny hair.

One final comment about Joy Rides: All too often, a woman will start a Joy Ride relationship and then decide that what began as a fling is now going to become a serious, marriage-bound relation-

The *Potential Mate* doesn't dance—or if he does, he shouldn't.

ship. Suddenly, this woman wants to train her *Joy Rider* to act like a *Potential Mate.* Impossible? Sometimes, but not always. Difficult? Exceptionally so. It's terribly hard to teach a man to say "Thank you" after he's already zipped up his pants and marched out the door.

Quiz

One of the men shown below is a *Potential Mate.* The other two are *Joy Riders.* Can you spot the *Potential Mate?*

(B is the *Potential Mate.*)

CHAPTER 4

When Good Men Do Bad Things

Men are superb creatures. But some of their day-to-day behavior can be quite vexsome—if not downright disgusting. Naturally, you will want to cure your man (or men, given your circumstances) of these behavioral perculiarities as quickly as possible.

The Lovehouse Woman must realize that *every* man needs and values a certain amount of mastery. His mother, if she was at all bright or intuitively adept, understood this. So, my dears, should you. A man, like any pet, should experience a certain amount of "righteous fear."

Many women, out of their own insecurity or naive good intentions, let their man get away with disobedience. This is a very bad idea. A man, like a dog, wants someone he can respect. *No* man can respect a woman who tolerates rudeness, infidelity, dirty habits, or lack of consideration for her feelings. Remember: Should your man suddenly resort to this type of behavior, it may be a last desperate ploy to rouse you into being the type of woman he can respect.

Remember: Respect and a certain "righteous fear" are two of the cornerstones of the Lovehouse Training Philosophy. Once these cornerstones have been laid in place, the continuation of training can proceed quite smoothly.

Especially important: When your man has done right, give him the wildest show of affection and a good romp. I cannot say this too often. Giving praise and affection is where so many women fail their men.

The Bad Things Men Do

WHAT YOUR MAN DOES WRONG

He goes golfing Sunday mornings and leaves you alone.

THE LOVEHOUSE SOLUTION

BALLS

Take away his balls.

He expects you to bend over when pouring beer and serving snacks.

Stand up straight when pouring his beer.

WHAT YOUR MAN DOES WRONG

He makes passes at you on the first date.

THE LOVEHOUSE SOLUTION

Show him you're the sort of woman that men respect.

What Your Man Does Wrong	*The Lovehouse Solution*
He covers everything he eats with mounds of ketchup.	Each day, add several drops of Tabasco sauce to the ketchup bottle in your refrigerator. Shake up the bottle. Naturally, you'll want to keep track of the dosage, because you'll want to similarly "improve" each new bottle that enters your home.
He leaves the toilet seat up.	I adore my husband Hercules. . . . He's a wonderful lover, a good provider, and a fine, warm, honest human being. But despite my experience and his basic desire to please, I could *not* succeed in training him to put that seat back down. . . . Then, one horribly cold night (I'll spare you the details) the solution came to me in a flash! Hercules *loathes* John Philip Sousa marches. The very next day, when Hercules went off to work, I hired a local handyman to create exactly the device I needed. The handyman, God bless him, rigged a timer and a portable tape deck to the toilet seat. It was installed by nightfall, and was well worth the price. . . . To this day, if more than 80 seconds pass, and that seat is not down, an automatic timer switches on John Philip Sousa marches—*loud.* (Hercules hardly *ever* forgets, these days, to put that seat back down.)
You think he may be seeing another woman. Fidelity is very important to you. He says you're	When in doubt, check it out: Hire a private detective. In the case of love, it is not out of line, despite

the only woman in his life, but somehow you just don't believe him.

what the Supreme Court says, to tap his phone, bug his office, steam open his mail, or put a homing device on his car.

The love of your life comes home from work, eats dinner, and plunks himself in front of the TV set for the evening. You are starved for conversation.

This is an extremely common problem, with quite a simple solution. Tomorrow morning, remove at least one tube from every TV set in your house. If you have sets without tubes, just dig in and pull some wires. Or go outside and cut the cable-TV connection. When the repairman comes, bribe him to say he has to order a part from the factory, and it'll take at least two weeks.

He talks too much when he meets new people because he's nervous.

There is one surefire cure for nerves: Valium. Five to 10 milligrams dissolved in a glass of fresh-squeezed orange juice ought to do the trick. (Do make sure he doesn't drink any alcohol while you're out.) Your friends and business associates may find your man dull—but better a boring man than a foolish one.

Your lover snores.

Men tend to snore when they lie flat on their back (it's just a peculiarity of the breed). If you cannot train your mate to respond to the command "Roll over," simply prick him sharply with a sewing needle kept discreetly on your bedside table. He will automatically change positions and stop snoring.

He brings home unplanned guests and expects you to cook and clean up after them.

Discreetly slip away from hubby and guests. Go down to the basement and turn off the master power switch. (Don't worry, the food in your freezer will not melt.)

Cheerily reappear, lit candle in hand, and say, "There must be a temporary power failure. Why don't we go out to dinner . . . " (Apartment dwellers need only unscrew one or two fuses to get the same results.)

He keeps insisting that he'd like to have sex with you and another woman at the same time.	Enlist the aid of your fattest aunt. Invite her to stay over for the night. See that she wears nice pink rollers in her hair, blue eyeshadow, and a cute peignoir set. Say to your love privately, over a glass of wine, "Well here's your chance. . . . You wanted to make love to me and another woman at the same time. Aunt Sophie is willing . . . "
He tells horrible ethnic or sexist jokes. You've asked him not to, but he won't stop.	Buy copies of all the *Gross Jokes* books you can find. Memorize all the jokes that apply to *his* ethnic group. One night when you're out in company, regale his friends with at least one hour of disgusting jokes about the Irish (if he's Irish), WASPs (if he's a WASP), etc.
He decides to run for political office.	No woman deserves to be the wife of a politician: Your husband will never be home; he'll meet too many attractive women; and your past will become a matter of public record. Naturally, desperate measures are called for. . . . You *must*, without scruples or hesitation, search your memory for the one scandal or shady deal he was involved in (think back—there must be something), and call the journalist of your choice with the appropriate information.

He's suddenly gotten "beauty" conscious and keeps using extraordinary amounts of your expensive night cream. You've asked him to stick to his own Oil of Olay, but he says he likes yours better.

Scoop out your face cream and place it in an unmarked container. Replace the expensive cream with Crisco. Smooth the top so it looks like a new jar. When he complains about the cream, say, "Oh, they must have changed the formula . . . "

He wears the same socks or underwear more than one day in a row.

Incredible as it may seem, some men, especially men who have lived too long alone, have this revolting habit. It *must not* be tolerated. The *moment* you see your love pup heading toward yesterday's underwear, summon every inch of courage in you and say, "Do *not* put those on!" If you must, grab them out of his hands and put them in the hamper.

He makes love to you with morning (bad) breath.

Most men sleep with their mouths open. This is, for our purposes, most convenient. The *moment* you waken, grab the Binaca from your bedside drawer and spray into his mouth.

He doesn't bathe often enough.

This is a problem I have never personally encountered. But readers of my weekly syndicated column, "Training Men the Lovehouse Way," do write to me over and over again about this loathsome situation. As I see it, there are only two solutions. One, offer to give your man a nice bubble bath as part of your precoital play. Or, if you have the figure for it, offer to shower with him. Two, unless he bathes, you *must* refuse to have sex with him. . . . As you well know, this is a solution I abhor. But I don't see any way around it. Besides, really, who could abide anything else?

He doesn't kiss your neck enough while you're making love.	While your man is in the midst of coital pleasure, say firmly and authoritatively, "Kiss my neck . . . " If necessary, repeat the command. If he does not respond, eliminate him from your life. A man who does not kiss your neck while making love to you is not worth keeping.

A Special Note About Dirty and Untidy Men

As you will have determined from the previous few pages, men do have some *awful* habits. But how did they get that way? And what can *we* do about it? It is my conviction that, for better or for worse, most of a man's pivotal training takes place in the first eight years of his development. My techniques, naturally, can redirect and change certain types of behavior—but chances are that if his dear mom cleaned up after him and allowed sloppy behavior during those first eight years (or longer), you are facing a *very* formidable training task.

One cannot fully blame his mom, though. In our culture the birth of a male child is an extraordinary event that confirms the virility of the father, and is a virtual guarantee (unless the child develops into a Poodle) that the family name will be perpetuated. Even today's suffragettes—er, liberationists—will make quite a fuss over the birth of a female child; yet, as anyone who has witnessed a family's reaction to the birth of a *male* child will attest, the birth of a *boy* is a very special event indeed.

Luckily, in my many years of training dogs, not all of whom came to me as puppies, I did discover certain general principles that work equally well with men. To review:

I. Most men are born normal. They are made abnormal by their upbringing.
II. Too many women are overly romantic and unable to deliver firm, clear commands. They end up with moody men, disagreeable men, roving men, disobedient men—to say nothing of *dirty* men.
III. Often, men simply do not *hear*

the female voice. It is high, it is soft, it's so *feminine*. Remember, a man only understands a harsh, loud, *immediate* command.

IV. Always praise generously when he behaves.

Memorize the points above. Make them part of your basic world view.

Still, my In-box remains full of letters from women in love who, to their disgust and chagrin, find that the man in their life has certain annoying or unsanitary habits. Let's consider, for example:

Clothing on the Floor. In the beginning of a relationship, especially during the heat of passion, clothing will wind up on the floor. Darlings, if you'll be honest with yourselves, haven't there been times when *your* clothing, under these special circumstances, wound up on the floor, too? Thus, be tolerant of your man the first time he throws his clothes. However, the second time it happens, Lovehouse Neatness Training must commence. One solution is the direct question: Why don't we hang up our clothing? What man, even an amorously overzealous one, would refuse you such a simple request? *Remember to praise.* Do *not* offer to hang up clothing for *both* of you, because this will reinforce a bad habit: You will become mummy-who-cleans-up-after-me.

Fine, you may say, I can see that working during moments of passion . . . but you don't know my pet.

Every time he undresses, he lets his clothing fall to the floor and leaves it there. Well, this is a slightly different case.

The habitually messy man does present a certain challenge. Yet, even a confirmed slob *can* be trained. There are, as I see it, five approaches to this problem.

1. **Correct Your Pup.** *Immediately,* when you see that clothing hit the floor, in a firm, authoritative voice, say, "Messy boy!" (This is pronounced "meessy boy"; draw out those "e's".) "Pick up your clothing!" Do not scream. Do not whine. Be very professional in your command. Remember, your man likes a little mastery. Very good. Now, praise, praise, praise.

2. **Bell Therapy.** My darling Aunt Maude, who had a lovely farm in Sussex, always summoned the family to meals by vigorously sounding the old cowbell she kept hanging by the kitchen door for that purpose. How the sound of that bell carried! Several years back, when the farm became too much for her, Auntie Maude was kind enough to give me that bell. I suggest that you acquire one for yourself. Now, when your love drops his clothing on the floor, pick up that bell and *ring it as loud as you can.* Very good. Counterbalance the harsh tone of the bell by saying, liltingly and melodiously, "Cleanup time!" Now, praise, praise, praise.

3. *Pal-to-Pal Concept.* Here, one chooses a quiet, mellow moment, perhaps a romantic interlude before the fireplace, with quiet music and a soothing glass of sherry or cognac. One says, "You know, I love you very much." (Pet your man as you say this.) "But there are certain little habits you have that threaten to undermine our relationship." If you are a believer in psychotherapeutic banter, I'm sure you can take it from there . . .

4. *Hire a Maid.* Sometimes, in very tough cases, the techniques outlined above fail. This is the time to hire a maid. Let her (or him) pick up, sort, and put away or wash your man's clothing. *You* are not your man's mommy; it's not your job.

5. *Find Someone Neater.* If clothing on the floor (usually accompanied by other slobby behavior) truly bothers you, and the techniques I've mentioned do not work, you may have to consider finding someone else to love—a military man, for example.

Take It From Barbara: More Lovehouse Solutions

What Your Man Does Wrong	*The Lovehouse Solution*
He doesn't put the cap back on the tube of toothpaste.	Remove the radiator cap from his car. Refuse to return it until your man replaces the toothpaste cap.
He wolfs his food. You suspect he doesn't even taste it.	Put some Alpo on one of your prettier dishes. Place it on the kitchen table or counter. Begin preparing lunch, but don't get at all far. Say, "Honey, I have to run to the grocery to get something. I'll be right back." When you return and find the Alpo eaten, inform your greedy love that he's just consumed the dog's dinner.

He's still reading Marvel comic books. He's especially fond of "The Hulk."

Invite your most outrageous male homosexual friend to dinner. Have him exclaim, "Oh my God! I thought only drag queens still read 'The Hulk!' "

He drinks coffee incessantly but almost never washes the pot.

Be sure that you use an automatic percolator. Use the same grounds over and over and over again. Do not wash the pot, either. When he complains about the coffee, say "Oh, why don't you make a fresh pot. Yours comes out so much better than mine."

He talks in his sleep. It wakes you up, and besides, he won't answer your questions.

Tape his mouth shut.

When he finishes a meal, he licks the plate. He rarely if ever does this in front of anyone but you.

Have a self-focusing flash camera ready. The *moment* plate meets tongue, take the shot. Develop the film immediately. (Hide the negatives.) Tell him if you see him do this again, you will show the picture to all his most sophisticated friends.

He thrashes in his sleep. You're black-and-blue from flailing arms and legs.

Allow him to fall asleep. Then tie him up.

He complains bitterly about the time it takes you to get ready to go out.

Wait until there's an important occasion scheduled, something that's important to him (a business function or the wedding of his cousin Alvin). Make sure that you stay up reading the night before so that you have nice, puffy dark circles under your eyes. Don't wash or set your hair. Say to him, about two hours before you're scheduled to leave, "Honey, I know how it bothers you that it takes me so long to get ready . . . Well, tonight I'm going to be ready in no time at all . . ." Do not bathe. Do not put on makeup. Throw on a pair of Bermuda shorts. Even if your darling makes you go as you are, rest assured he'll never complain about your preparation time again.

He expects you to account for every minute of time you don't spend with him.	Make a daily diary sheet, broken down into 5-minute segments. Spend two days keeping very close account of your time. Be sure to enter things like "went to bathroom," and "bought shoe polish." Give him your diary sheets, plus seven blank ones of his own. Tell him that if he expects such close accounting of *your* time, you expect the same from him. (If you *receive* diary sheets from him, you undoubtedly have a Basset Hound on your hands.)
You're a great cook. It offends you that your partner automatically salts his food before tasting it.	Put sugar in your salt shaker.
He bites his nails.	Put polish on them while he sleeps.
Your darling sang so badly as a child they wouldn't let him in his elementary-school glee club. Yet every time he steps into the shower, he sings—loudly and off-key. You can't take it another minute.	One of your friends must have a dog that howls or barks incessantly. Take a tape recorder to your friend's house, and tape the offending racket. Whenever your love enters the shower, sneak in after him with a portable tape player. The *moment* he begins to sing, play the tape at full volume. Your love may not be happy, but at least he'll stop singing . . .

He doesn't put milk or other perishables back in the refrigerator.

Leave the milk on the counter until he wants it again. Serve him the milk. When he complains that it's sour, explain why . . .

CHAPTER 5

Dr. Barbara Lovehouse's 7-Day No-Nonsense Shape-Up Plan

A successful and happy graduate of my training program.

Every night, millions of American women come home to a sullen, hungry, demanding man whose welcoming words are "What's for dinner?" Contrast that with the lucky female who owns a dog. That woman receives an enthusiastic, loving reception. The little doggie doesn't notice her housekeeping or even what she's wearing. All he knows is that his mistress is home again, and all's right with the world!

Yet all that stands between the grateful dog and the ungrateful man is proper training!

Now, as I've said before, many women fear the idea of training, and worry that it will ruin their man. But the ruined man is the *un-trained* man who belongs to an oversentimental owner. An untrained man lacks all respect for his mistress and refuses to perform even the simplest of tasks.

During my years of training I have managed to synthesize the most important elements of my teaching into a crash "7-Day Shape-Up Plan." With this simple plan your well-trained man will become a faithful companion, an eager and willing playmate, a resourceful lover, and, if desired, a model husband.

If you are truly committed, almost any man can be completely trained in seven days. This takes dedication and concentration. It also takes a man.

Where to Meet Trainable Men	**Where NOT to Meet Trainable Men**
Mercedes-Benz showrooms	Toys "R" Us
Funeral parlors (an excellent source for the newly widowed)	Bridal shops
Better men's clothing stores	Judy Garland film festivals
Yacht clubs	Obstetricians' waiting rooms

It used to be easy to recognize a trainable man by certain qualities. These days, unfortunately, many of these qualities have been vastly underrated, whereas others are valued far above their true worth. In order to help you select a trainable man, I offer some overrated and underrated qualities.

Overrated Qualities	Underrated Qualities
A sense of humor	A trade
A social conscience	A pension plan
Good looks	Good credit rating
Sexuality	A desire to please
Dark, wavy hair	A brain
Masculinity	Generosity

Basic Training

Before you take your man through the ropes of my 7-day shape-up plan, you need to familiarize yourself with certain basic principles and rules.

All of my training can be summed up in three short statements. Memorize them:

The Three Principles of Man Training

1. **Praise good behavior *immediately*.**
2. **Punish bad behavior *immediately*.**
3. **No wire coat hangers, *ever*.**

Sound simple? It should be. Unfortunately, men are cunning creatures. While *they* know when they're being bad, they will do anything to keep *you* from knowing. This leads us to my first rule of basic training:

Lovehouse Rule #1: Know the difference between good and bad behavior. Men are fond of hiding their bad actions behind good ones. Why

do they do this? To drive you crazy. How do they do this? Read the following list and see if you can find the bad actions hidden behind the good ones:

1. **Good** He gives you a lovely black dress . . .

   Bad . . . but it's four sizes too large . . .

   Worse . . . and has sweat dripping from the armholes.

2. ***Good***   He takes you to a great party . . .

   Bad   . . . but flirts with the hostess . . .

   Worse   . . . who is pregnant with his child.

3. ***Good***   He gives you flowers . . .

   Bad   . . . that are wilted . . .

   Worse   . . . because he stole them off a grave.

4. ***Good***   He tells you that you look beautiful . . .

   Bad   . . . but exhausted . . .

   Worse   . . . and so he's not going to take you out tonight.

5. ***Good***   He asks you to marry him . . .

   Bad   . . . someday . . .

   Worse   . . . when his wife dies.

Now that you know the difference between good and bad behavior, it's time to learn how to reward a man for good behavior and punish him for bad behavior:

Lovehouse Rule #2: The best way to reward or punish a man is through his sense of touch. Unfortunately, men do not particularly care whether you ever say "I love you." They would much rather have a woman *show* her love than *speak* her love. This is due to a certain amount of mental weakness on the part of men.

Men, like dogs, enjoy being petted and fear being struck.

To Reward Your Man, Touch Him Gently in these Important Places:

The inner thigh
The curve of the neck
The upper back
His ears
His privates
His nipples
Any prominent muscles

To Punish Your Man, Touch Him Gently in These Important Places:

His eyeballs
The skin under his fingernails
The inside of his nostrils
His liver
His tonsils
His eardrums

Lovehouse Rule #3: Do not reward a man when guilt, as opposed to love, is inspiring his good behavior. Men are most likely to be good the minute after they have been bad. Just as the dog will come to you wagging his tail after he's wet your finest Oriental rug, the man will come running to you with a fur coat after he's crawled out of bed with your best friend.

The Barbara Lovehouse Guilt Chart

- If your man buys you a trench coat . . .

  . . . he is thinking about sleeping with another woman.

- If your man buys you a raccoon coat . . .

  . . . he is thinking about how much fun he had sleeping with another woman.

- If your man buys you a mink coat . . .

  . . . he is thinking about how much fun he had sleeping with another man.

- If your man buys you a sable coat . . .

  . . . you don't want to know.

Other Signs That Your Man Is Feeling Guilty

1. He suddenly suggests that the two of you spend the weekend visiting your parents.
2. He cries when you say that you trust him.
3. You receive a large, expensive bouquet of flowers from him (he *never* sends flowers) with a card that reads, "You are the best thing that ever happened to me."
4. He suggests that you and your girlfriend (one of the ones he usually criticizes) take a nice, long vacation together to Bermuda. He'll pay.
5. He gives you a large gift of cash and tells you to buy whatever you'd like.

About My Plan

Ideally, my plan is designed for a week during which you can devote all your time and concentration to training. The two of you should put your careers and other responsibilities on hold and focus totally on training. I promise you the results will be well worth it.

As you will see, this 7-Day Shape-Up Plan is designed for couples who already have a relationship. But I believe it can work wonders for anyone. If, for example, the two of you are not already married or living together, it may be difficult to begin every day at 8:30 A.M. A truly committed woman, however, will see to it that she gets the keys to her man's apartment and shows up there at 8:30 A.M. When the program is completed, he'll thank you for it.

Other adjustments become a matter of personal taste. You may, for example, prefer to have your sex session early in the day, and your exercise hour late at night. After the 7-Day program is completed, I recommend constant review of the training principles. You may find that your man needs more work in some areas than others. So be it. No one is better qualified to train him than you.

Your Man's Typical Day . . .
Before the Lovehouse 7-Day Shape-Up Plan

9:00 A.M.   He asks you to call his boss to say he's sick . . . again.

10:00 A.M.   He is served waffles in bed: "Did you warm the syrup, honey?"

11:00 A.M.   He burps.

12:00 P.M.	He stops at the local tavern for "one" drink.
3:00 P.M.	He burps.
5:00 P.M.	He takes a nap before calling his bookie.
6:00 P.M.	He is served a gourmet dinner by you, but is too hung over to eat.
7:00 P.M.	He tells you about a friend of his who left his wife for a younger woman.
7:01 P.M.	He asks you how old you are.
7:02 P.M.	He asks you whether you think young women find him attractive.
7:03 P.M.	He leaves home "for a newspaper."
2:00 A.M.	You cry yourself to sleep ... alone.

Your Man's Typical Day ...
(*After* the Lovehouse 7-Day Shape-Up Plan)

8:00 A.M.	Morning sex warm-up (optional).
8:30 A.M.	He rises to prepare breakfast.
9:00 A.M.	He serves you breakfast in bed.
9:30 A.M.	He cleans up the kitchen.
10:00 A.M.	He makes the bed, vacuums the rugs, and dusts.
12:00 P.M.	He prepares lunch.
12:30 P.M.	He serves you lunch.
1:30 P.M.	Afternoon sex break (optional).
2:30 P.M.	He does the grocery shopping, picks up your clothes from the cleaners, etc.
4:30 P.M.	He prepares afternoon tea.
5:30 P.M.	He gives you a relaxing massage, then while you nap he puts away the groceries, etc.
7:00 P.M.	He prepares for dinner out.
8:00 P.M.	He shares a romantic candlelit dinner with you.
10:00 P.M.	Evening sex break.
1:00 A.M.	Before dropping off to sleep, he thanks the Lord he found a woman who would train him.

Day 1
Today's Goal:
Getting His Attention

Getting your man's attention can be a real challenge whether you are dealing with a longtime lover or a total stranger who just stepped out of a Porsche 910. For proper training to begin, you must have his complete attention. He can't be distracted by anything or anyone, especially not by that Morgan Fairchild look-alike who just moved in next door.

I recommend these attention-grabbers:

1. *Lock Up The TV.* If your man would rather watch Monday night football than sit up and pay attention to training, you have no choice.

2. *Hide His Clothes.* This is best done while he is sleeping or in the shower. This will prevent him from sneaking off to some local tavern to watch Monday night football there.

3. *Tie Him Up.* A good tight leash never hurt anyone and will help you control your man during the initial training period. Occasionally, you will run across a man who *enjoys* being tied up and takes it as a prelude to sex play. So much the better.

4. *Throw Some Water On Him.* Yes, a good hosing will have the effect of a nice cold shower, bringing your man back to reality and to you. I recommend carrying a small water pistol at all times. A few "spritzes" will refresh your man and remind him about his training.

Day 2
Today's Goal:
Learning the
Pleasures of Dating

I define a date as any nonsexual experience the two of you can share away from home and for which the man pays all expenses. I do not consider "Dutch treat" dates worthy of discussion.

Dates	*Nondates*
A day at the beach	A day at his mother's
A trip to the movies	A trip to the unemployment office
Dinner in a nice restaurant	Dinner at Taco Bell
A night at a Rolling Stones concert	A night of his playing the guitar for you
A drive in the country with a stop for lunch at a romantic little restaurant	A drive downtown to pick up some discount auto parts for his car

I have known women who have lived with men five years or longer, yet who have never introduced their men to Date Training. Did they expect him to discover it himself?

Today's Exercise: Picking Up The Check. A man who has never picked up a check in his life may not know where to begin. When the check arrives, rise and announce that you are about to visit the powder room and will meet him outside (restaurants usually have a vestibule or small hall for this purpose). Even better, before the check arrives, excuse yourself for the powder room and on the way let the maitre d' know that your man wants the check. Do *not* return to the table until he has paid, even if this means you are forced to spend a night sleeping in a bathroom.

Advanced Exercise: Giving You $20 "For The Washroom Attendant." Has your man ever been inside the ladies' room of an expensive restaurant? Probably not—and what he doesn't know won't hurt him. During the course of your meal, make frequent complaints about the expenses involved in visiting the ladies' room. Tell him how one must pay for use of the toilet paper, the stall, the garbage can, the mirror, etc. When it comes time for you to visit the ladies' room, sigh first, then say, "Just give me a twenty."

Day 3
Today's Goal: Learning the Pleasures of Trained Sex

The first question I'm usually asked about sex is "How much is too much?" Whether you enjoy making love three times a day or on New Year's Eve only, it's up to you to set the amount of sex you and your man will have. He'll respect you for it.

It is, of course, perfectly proper for your man to initiate sex, but he must learn the correct way to do it.

Proper Ways to Introduce Sex	*Improper Ways to Introduce Sex*
Let's make love.	Want to earn an easy five bucks?
Let me help you find your G Spot.	Got a minute?

Today's Exercise: Exploring Your Body. Although most men begin kissing women when in their early teens and start intercourse shortly afterward, many of them never get to the stop-offs in-between. This is somewhat akin to visiting New York and Los Angeles and believing that you have seen all of America. To train him to make those stop-offs in-between, I suggest taking a felt pen and marking a dotted line from your lips to the crook of your ear to the base of your neck and downwards, so that he understands the scenic route his little tongue should take. It might even be helpful to indicate the time expected at each stop; for example, 10 minutes on your lips, 20 minutes on each breast, etc.

Post-Sex Training. Don't neglect this important phase of Sex Training. The key to post-sex behavior is the phone call. Soon after you have been together, it is appropriate for the man to telephone the woman and express his gratitude.

Exactly how soon after is flexible. One's husband or live-in lover, for example, should call immediately. An astronaut, on the other hand, may not have access to a phone immediately. Nevertheless, the call should come within 48 hours. A call within one week is acceptable. A call after six months is acceptable only if he has been the hostage of a revolutionary government.

Two Words That Will Immeasurably Improve Your Sex Life

"Me first."

Day 4
Today's Goal: Domestication

The properly domesticated man is devoted to home life and household affairs. He is easy to recognize.

The Domesticated Man	The Undomesticated Man
Wakes you by asking "How would you like your eggs?"	Wakes you by asking "What's your name?"
Never runs out of coffee, tea, or steam.	Never runs out of excuses.
Always cleans the tub after he uses it.	Doesn't know where the tub is.
Picks up after himself.	Picks his nose.
Wears clean, sexy underwear.	Wears no underwear.
Thinks snow is to shovel.	Thinks snow is to snort.
Is equally at home in the bedroom or the kitchen.	Is never home.

Today's Exercise: Cleaning House. Introduce your man to the pleasures of vacuuming the house. Explain that Pete Rose keeps in shape by vacuuming. Confide that Ron Dugay relaxes by making beds. Announce that the sight of a clean kitchen makes you hot.

Day 5
Today's Goal:
Understanding the Pleasures of Exercise & Play

Every man must be exercised regularly. If he isn't, he'll become bored, restless, and depressed. In such a state, there's no telling what kind of mischief he might get into. Now is the time to build a regular exercise program. Although he may resist at first, your man will soon look forward to walks in the better shopping areas. Is there any sight happier than that of a well-trained man frolicking along Fifth Avenue, Michigan Avenue, or Rodeo Drive?

As a responsible woman, it's up to you to provide the right kind of stimulation. Some examples:

The Right Kind of Stimulation

Jewelry stores

Menus in fine restaurants

Fur salons

Travel brochures

Architectural Digest

The Wrong Kind of Stimulation

Beauty contests

Gambling casinos

Racetracks

Club Med

Playboy

Today's Exercise: Museum Visiting. Walking your man through a large museum will provide a wealth of stimulation and exercise for him. You can make the most of the visit by reading the museum catalog in advance. Start him off in the precious gems area, introducing him to the stones that mean the most to you. Next stop off in the costume collection so that he can see the kind of clothes you are interested in receiving. This is also a good spot to introduce him to potential fantasies the two of you can act out, such as "Gable & Lombard" or "Catherine the Great and her favorite thoroughbred."

THERE ARE CERTAIN CULTURAL EXPERIENCES YOU MAY NOT WANT YOUR MAN TO HAVE.

Day 6
Today's Goal:
Introduction to Verbal Communication

An important difference between men and dogs is that a dog cannot be trained to say "I love you." Your man can and should say these words. There are other "sweet nothings" a woman would like to hear also, just as there are a few things she would rather *never* hear.

Some Things a Woman Likes to Hear	*Some Things a Woman Doesn't Like to Hear*
My ex-wife has custody of the kids.	Have you gained weight?
What good is money if you don't spend it?	It wasn't just a cold sore after all.
You wait here. I'll go get the Mercedes.	What's your sister's phone number?
I just *love* waxing floors.	I'm a little short on cash this week.
Can I change the diapers? Please?	My last girlfriend was terrific except for one thing: she wanted to get married.

Dr. Barbara Lovehouse's Foolproof Way to Get Your Man to Say "I Love You."

1. **Hold a carving knife to his crotch.**
2. **Lock him in his room without dinner or TV.**
3. **Tell him the words make you hot.**

When he does say "I love you," smother him with kisses and praise, praise, praise. Thus reinforced, he'll find it much easier to say next time.

Today's Exercise: Strengthening the Tongue. While we are dealing with things oral, let's take the time to build up that tongue. A man's tongue should be as agile as an Olympic athlete, as sensuous as a snake. The emphasis here is on strength and control. Begin by having him lift a paper clip off a table. (Remember, the goal here is *not* speed.) A champion tongue should eventually be able to hold an entire roll of quarters without flinching.

Day 7
Today's Goal: Showing and Performance in Public

Day 7 is divided into two parts. The daytime hours are devoted to allowing your man to perform on his own without being closely supervised by you. In the evening hours you will bring him out for a showing.

For the last six days you and your man have been inseparable as you put him through his paces. Now is the time to take a little breather from each other. Feel free to leave your man at home while you go out for an intimate little lunch with "an old friend." Your well-trained man will be eager to show how well he's learned his lessons. By the time you return in the afternoon he should be waiting in the doorway, water for tea on the boil. Allow him to take you on a tour of the house so that he can show off his work. Remember to praise, praise, praise the made beds, the tidy bathroom, and the sparkling kitchen. Don't expect perfection yet (only practice makes perfect), but don't hesitate to point out lapses and correct them immediately. If your man has forgotten, for example, to empty the bathroom wastebasket, point to it, and say, "No, no, no." He'll get the idea.

After you share the tea he has

prepared, suggest that he give you a soothing massage. That will make you ready for a restful nap while your man washes the tea cups and draws your bath.

This evening you'll be introducing your newly trained man to the arena of life, by bringing him to such unstructured events as large parties. Where formerly you would have quaked with fear that your man, confused by the scent of so many strange perfumes, might follow the wrong woman home, you can now be sure he'll stick close to your side.

Dealing with Separation Anxiety. Sometimes, if circumstances call your man away from your side, he will show the symptoms of "separation anxiety" by wildly moving from woman to woman as he searches for you (or a close approximation of you). It is at this time that he's most vulnerable to bitches in heat. Often the only solution is the water pistol. A few squirts will cool him off and bring him back to reality.

Today's Trick: Bonding. It's important for women to know that your man belongs to you, but a collar and a license are usually inappropriate. Instead, when the two of you go out for the evening, carry the most feminine evening purse you have. As soon as you arrive, hand it to him. This will clearly mark your man as taken.

CHAPTER 6

How to Identify Your Man's Breed: A Quiz

BASSET
HOUND

GREAT
DANE

ST.
BERNARD

WOLF

POODLE

One crucial aspect of the Lovehouse Method is selecting the breed that's right for you. I have found that in general men can be divided into five breeds: Wolves, Poodles, Great Danes, St. Bernards, and Basset Hounds. This simple quiz will help you to determine what category of man you are dealing with.

---

1. **You arrive at a party together. He immediately**
   - (a) Flirts with an attractive woman.
   - (b) Flirts with an attractive man.
   - (c) Is approached by people who want advice about their investments, marriages, and/or vacation plans.
   - (d) Is asked to mix drinks.
   - (e) Is asked to leave.

2. **His favorite drink is**
   - (a) Your blood.
   - (b) A Pink Lady—Mother loves them, too.
   - (c) Beefeater martini or Johnny Walker Black—no ice, no explanations.
   - (d) Budweiser beer—the colder the better.
   - (e) Tang—the drink of the astronauts.

3. **He invites you home to see his video tape player. The first tape he shows you is**
   - (a) "Deep Loving" with Marilyn Chambers and Harry Reams.
   - (b) The Best of the Judy Garland Show.
   - (c) "The MacNeil-Lehrer News Hour."
   - (d) The only episode of "Dallas" that you ever missed.
   - (e) The Best of "The Beverly Hillbillys."

4. **Peeking into his refrigerator, you'll find**
   - (a) Half of a beautiful peach pie with "I love you" still readable on the crust and a half-empty bottle of champagne—celebrating something you know nothing about.
   - (b) A container of low-fat cottage cheese and the entire Elizabeth Arden Millenium line.
   - (c) Nothing—his expense account covers three meals.
   - (d) Instant coffee, a bottle of catsup, a bag of English muffins or bagels, and a bar of chocolate.
   - (e) Something green and smelly.

5.   On a dinner date, he probably has no idea that
   (a) You have never gone braless before.
   (b) You'd rather be with someone else.
   (c) You don't understand any of the French on the menu.
   (d) You will be fasting tomorrow.
   (e) You have never been to McDonald's before.

6.   As a little boy he dreamed of becoming
   (a) A lifeguard surrounded by big-breasted, bikini-clad women.
   (b) A fashion designer surrounded by anorexic models.
   (c) Secretary of the Treasury Department. (Of course, he wouldn't have minded being President of the United States, either.)
   (d) A fireman, policeman, or secret agent.
   (e) A mailman—he always wanted to travel.

7.   These days, he'd like to be
   (a) Warren Beatty.
   (b) Calvin Klein.
   (c) No one but himself.
   (d) A father.
   (e) Anyone but himself.

8.   His favorite sex symbol is
   (a) This month's Penthouse Pet.
   (b) Richard Gere.
   (c) Katherine Hepburn.
   (d) You.
   (e) Miss Piggy.

9.   He likes a woman who
   (a) Understands that a man has needs.
   (b) Can take criticism.
   (c) Shows good breeding.
   (d) Likes children and pets.
   (e) Is disease-free.

10.   If his life were a movie, it would be called
   (a) *Everything You Always Wanted to Know About Sex, But Were Afraid to Ask.*
   (b) *The Virgin Queen.*
   (c) *The Man in the Gray Flannel Suit.*
   (d) *The All-American Boy.*
   (e) *Lord of the Flies.*

11. He might surprise you with a getaway vacation to
- (a) Club Med, Martinique, where there are seven women to every man.
- (b) Key West, Florida, where there are seven men to every woman.
- (c) His summer home in Maine.
- (d) The Grand Canyon.
- (e) His family's place on the Love Canal.

12. His favorite sexual fantasy
- (a) Involves more than one woman.
- (b) Takes place on a yacht off the coast of Mykonos.
- (c) Doesn't exist—he's a *doer* not a *dreamer.*
- (d) Involves you.
- (e) Involves losing his virginity.

13. He collects
- (a) Broken hearts.
- (b) Joan Rivers's prom pictures.
- (c) Stocks and bonds.
- (d) Friends.
- (e) Allergies.

14. He believes that the United States is a great country because
- (a) American girls have long legs and big breasts.
- (b) American men have strong legs and big chests.
- (c) The stock market is going up.
- (d) It's the land of the free and the home of the brave.
- (e) It hasn't asked him to leave . . . yet.

Scoring:
If the majority of your answers were
(a) You have a **Wolf.** This one's a heartache looking for a place to happen. He'll never give up the hunt. The best you can hope for is that age will slow him down in the chase. This is the hardest man to train.
(b) You have a **Poodle.** He has his uses, such as tips on clothes and interior decorating, but don't ever imagine that he can be trained for use in the bedroom. Also, his presence tends to discourage other breeds.

(c) You have a **Great Dane.** Reserved, well-bred, and self-disciplined, this man is *proud* of the fact that he hides his emotions. Deep down, the Great Dane is both shy and old-fashioned. He likes to live well but expects his woman to enjoy life on *his* terms.

(d) You have a **St. Bernard,** the salt of the earth. This man is so good, so loving, that sometimes you take him for granted. He may not be the best looking of the breeds, and your friends may be more impressed with a Wolf or a Great Dane, but there's none more loyal.

(e) You have a **Basset Hound,** but don't worry: Nothing is forever. He's invaluable for those situations when you *must* have a *male* escort; just don't let him talk to anybody.

CHAPTER 7

You and Your Wolf

This rogue is dedicated to the hunt. He is tireless, capable of working any terrain for new victims, yet is intensely jealous of the woman he calls his own. He can be restless and needs frequent, vigorous exercise in the bedroom. Sometimes he can be a tad too eager to make new friends, especially among females. He must always be closely supervised and never left alone.

Even the poorest Wolf is always impeccably dressed, and he always knows the right thing to say, which is whatever his prey of the moment wants to hear.

Always remember that although your Wolf may look civilized, beneath that expensive striped shirt beats the heart of a ruthless predator.

The Wolf suffers from a short attention span and frequently loses interest once a victim has been brought home. He must be constantly stimulated and amused. An untrained Wolf has a tendency to jump on female visitors. But his greatest fault is an urge to roam. Even in a good relationship he may suddenly feel this urge. Do not ignore the signs. Better to nip this immediately, or be prepared to lead a life of misery.

This animal will never give you a feeling of commitment, and even as he says "I do," he will be thinking "No, I don't." Yet, in spite of all the pain the Wolf delivers, women, including your best friends, will gladly do *anything* for him.

At Work and on the Road

You cannot expect to keep your Wolf in eye view at all times. That's why God created telephones. When business takes your Wolf on the road, see that he calls you every night. (Of course, that's no guarantee that he won't get off the phone with you and into bed with someone else; deviousness seems to make a Wolf horny.)

Also, leave little reminders of your love for him in surprising places. Finding a note from you in his wallet as he takes out his MasterCard to pay for some other woman's cocktails may have a dampening effect on any relationship—but of course, it's no guarantee.

Avoid letting him pack any particularly flattering clothes, like the blue shirt that matches his eyes. Go through his suitcase yourself and make these important adjustments. I always see that my man's favorite yellow tie is conveniently at the cleaner's when he's traveling without me.

How to Stop a Wolf from Flirting . . . Permanently

Wolves love to stalk fresh prey— especially at parties. If you're sick and tired of watching your Wolf flirt with sweet, young bunnies, follow these four simple steps. Your Wolf will *flirt no more.*

STEP ONE:

Wait until you catch your Wolf in the act of flirting.

Discreetly get his attention.

Quietly indicate your disapproval.

STEP FOUR:

Leave your man alone to think over the errors of his ways.

Marriage

The Wolf is not a breed well-suited for marriage. Proceed at your own peril.

What to Do When Your Wolf Has Roamed

Above all, do not storm out yourself or throw him out unless you want to end the relationship.

Let him know that you are hurt and feel betrayed. Cry. Cry a lot. Feel free to do this for an entire week, but no longer. (Remember that your Wolf has a short attention span.) Refuse to eat. (This is an excellent time to drop the 5 pounds you put on in happier days; besides, Wolves tend to be merciless about extra weight.) Do not discuss the details of the affair with him. You do not want to know the reasons why. In fact, with a Wolf, there probably *are* no reasons why . . .

Usually, by the third day of this, he'll be reduced to a whimpering cur. At this point, he'll be willing to do almost anything to please you. You'll find him voluntarily emptying the garbage or doing the dishes. When you feel he's had enough punishment, allow yourself to be pleased with his efforts. Smile at the dishes in the drainer or the newly repaired front door. Stroke his back and say, "*Sometimes,* you're so good."

The next day, have an affair with his best friend.

Where to Find a Wolf of Your Own

The Wolf is everywhere (with the possible exception of San Francisco). You'll find him in corporate boardrooms, driving eighteen wheelers, and even in some beauty salons. Some Wolves, like the late John F. Kennedy, have become heads of state. To get your own Wolf, all you have to do is wear something sexy: a tight sweater, a see-through lace blouse, or a pair of purple spandex pants. Then, just stand still. He'll find you.

Famous Wolves

Warren Beatty
Sylvester Stallone
The entire Kennedy family (except Robert F.)
Lyndon Johnson
Michael Landon
Gregory Harrison
J. R. Ewing
Rick James
Jack Nicholson
All Rolling Stones
Norman Mailer

A Word About False Wolves

There are a few men who actually cultivate the public image of a Wolf, when in reality they're something quite different. Anthony Geary of "General Hospital" for example, is a Poodle in Wolf's clothing.

Can You Be Happy with a Wolf?

	True	False
1. I think jealousy is immature and childish.	☐	☐
2. I like knowing my man is attractive to other women.	☐	☐
3. Just because a man gets late-night phone calls and notes from other women doesn't mean he's sleeping with them.	☐	☐
4. Just because a man's sleeping with other women doesn't mean he loves them.	☐	☐
5. It's natural for a man to fool around with other women.	☐	☐
6. I enjoy going to places like the Playboy Club because I think I can learn a lot from the bunnies.	☐	☐
7. Country Western music has a lot to say about male/female relationships.	☐	☐
8. I don't need to be the only woman in his life as long as I'm the most important.	☐	☐
9. All men fool around.	☐	☐
10. I'll never understand why Joan left Teddy.	☐	☐
11. I know he's had a bad record with other women, but it will be different with me.	☐	☐
12. I don't mind meeting a man's former lovers.	☐	☐
13. Just because he collects other women's phone numbers doesn't mean he is going to call them.	☐	☐
14. A man gives so much when making love, who can blame him if he forgets a girl's name.	☐	☐
15. I want a man with a *lot* of sexual experience.	☐	☐

Scoring:
If most of your answers were "True," you may be able to achieve something I thought was impossible: happiness with a Wolf. Good luck.

Clothes Make the Man

Isn't it nice to be with a man who knows he looks better than you do?

CHAPTER 8

You and Your Poodle

"WEARING THAT OLD THING AGAIN? NO WALKIES TONIGHT DEARIE!"

Your Poodle is a fun-loving sort and rapidly is becoming the most common breed, especially in large cities and interesting resort towns. The general rule about the Poodle is that he is seldom interested in more than companionship from a woman. He is extremely agile, especially on the dance floor, and he knows all kinds of clever ways for living creatively on next to nothing. Your poodle probably knows lots of sexual tricks, too, but most of them would be of little interest to you.

Your Poodle does have his weaknesses. He's often high-strung and given to whining. He can be quite snobbish, no matter how humble his own bloodlines are.

Ignoring celibacy, the main problem you will have with your Poodle is that he will often encourage your worst qualities, such as bitchiness. He will also praise eccentric styles that may turn off other breeds. Nevertheless, properly trained, he can be an excellent, devoted companion.

Training Your Poodle to Stay

Training your Poodle to stay with you is really no problem as long as there is no other woman in the room who is better-looking, more fashionably dressed, more famous, richer, in this month's *Vogue* or *Town & Country*, or the wife of someone rich and/or famous, or in the theater. Of course, a good-looking man in the room will distract the Poodle as well. If you insist on going out with a Poodle, do make sure you have cab fare in your purse.

At Work and on the Road

Poodles love to call long-distance, especially from someone else's phone. But do try to discourage collect calls. More important: *Do not*, under any circumstances, give the Poodle your telephone credit card number.

Marriage to the Poodle

Don't even think about it.

What to Do When Your Poodle Has Roamed

Invite them both to dinner.

Where to Find a Poodle of Your Own

Fire Island
San Francisco
Key West
New Orleans (the French Quarter)
New York (Greenwich Village, Soho)
Chicago (Lincoln Park)
Provincetown
Bucks County

Famous Poodles

Michael Jackson
Liberace
Elton John
Mr. Blackwell
Truman Capote
Richard Simmons
Charles Nelson Reilly

A Word About False Poodles

Very few men find it advantageous to masquerade as a Poodle. The exceptions are certain rock stars, such as David Bowie (a Great Dane in Poodle's clothing) and Mick Jagger (a Wolf if ever there was one).

Can You Find Happiness with a Poodle?

	True	False
1. I don't enjoy vigorous physical activity; it makes me sweaty and musses my hair.	☐	☐
2. Children bore me.	☐	☐
3. I think separate bedrooms are good for a marriage.	☐	☐
4. I've never understood the fuss about rock music. I'd much rather listen to show tunes and dance to disco.	☐	☐
5. If I ever find a hairdresser who really understands my hair, I'll do anything to keep him.	☐	☐
6. I am a rich old lady or plan to be.	☐	☐
7. Taste and sensitivity mean more to me than sex.	☐	☐
8. I can properly pronounce "Givenchy."	☐	☐
9. I need a man who knows the difference between Louis XIV and Louis XV.	☐	☐
10. I want to be a virgin when I die.	☐	☐

Scoring:
If most of your answers were "True" then perhaps you really will be happy with a Poodle.

Clothes Make the Man

You can share *everything* with your Poodle.

CHAPTER 9

You and Your Great Dane

"SO PLAN A SMALL DINNER PARTY FOR THIRTY BY FRIDAY."

Your Great Dane is an old-fashioned man. An excellent bread-
winner (he'd say that's a man's job),
he wants an old-fashioned woman,
one who is a lady, a good home-
maker, and a gracious hostess. The
Great Dane is a traditionalist, reserved in his attitude toward
women. You'll have to initiate
things and proceed cautiously. Try
not to let your Great Dane know
you are controlling his every move.

If you like fur coats and jewels,
this is the man for you. His woman
is a walking billboard that adver-
tises his worldly success.

More than any other breed, your
Great Dane is vulnerable to career
setbacks. Success means so much
to him that losing his job or a big
account can be devastating. It's
important for you to step in and
get that tail up and wagging as soon
as possible if you want him to continue fetching nice goodies.

Where to Find Your Great Dane

Great Danes can be found in pros-
perous cities including Boston, New
York (Manhattan), Washington,
D.C., Chicago (the Gold Coast), and
Cincinnati; you'll also find him in
exclusive resorts such as Palm
Springs, Hobe Sound, and Mar-
tha's Vineyard. Also check Rotary
Club meetings, airport VIP lounges,
country clubs, and tennis camps.

Warmth Training

Your Great Dane takes himself very
seriously and must be trained for
warmth and spontaneity. Surprise
him with a sexy card in his office
mail (make sure to mark it "personal"). Or, phone him during the
day to tell him that just the thought
of being together later is making
you hot. Proceed slowly and carefully.

Getting Your Great Dane to Say "I Love You"

It's often easier for a Great Dane
to give his woman a sapphire ring
than it is for him to say "I love you."
Although sapphire rings are nice,
there are times when a woman
needs romantic words. And for
those times, I have developed an
extremely successful method,
which I call a *"Je t'aime."*

Suggest that the two of you take
an Italian or French class together.
Perhaps you're planning to visit one
of these countries, or he has an important client who lives there. See
that one of the first phrases that
comes up in your homework is "I
love you." (You may have to con-
sult with your teacher on this, but
it's worth it.)

When he says *"Je t'aime"* or *"Ti
voglio bene,"* reply in English, "I
love you, too" and kiss him. You
may even wish to put aside the les-

son at this point. After repeating this exercise for several evenings, you'll find that the ice has been broken and your Great Dane will find saying "I love you" as easy as "Check please."

Training Your Great Dane for Spontaneity

Let's say that you would like your Great Dane to surprise you with champagne. Wait for an evening when he is supposed to take you to the movies. Have an almost empty bottle of good champagne on ice when he arrives. After you have drunk the two sips left in the bottle, tell him you're not interested in the movie anymore, the fact is that champagne makes you feel so sexy you can't keep your hands off him. When he reaches to kiss you, tell him you have sobered up and can *now* go to the movies. He should take it from there.

Celebrity Great Danes

Walter Mondale
Burt Lancaster
Robert Mitchum
Brian Keith
Walter Cronkite
Robert Young
Mike Wallace
Blake Carrington
Sidney Poitier
Ronald Reagan
Phil Donahue

A Word About False Great Danes

Sometimes Wolves, Poodles, and Basset Hounds will pretend to be Great Danes because they know you wouldn't bother with them if you knew what they really were. Even some misguided St. Bernards think they have to hide their true nature in order to impress you. Some well-known false Great Danes include:
Richard Nixon (a Basset Hound)
Johnny Carson (a Wolf)
Bob Hope (a Wolf)
Paul Newman (a St. Bernard)

Can You Find Happiness with a Great Dane?

	True	False
1. I'd love to trade places with Barbara Sinatra or Nancy Reagan.	☐	☐
2. America is a great country where anyone can get rich if he's willing to work at it—or if she's willing to support a man who wants to.	☐	☐
3. I don't want to be a queen; I just want to live like one.	☐	☐
4. I never get tired of hearing about my man's business.	☐	☐
5. Something worth buying is worth having in every color.	☐	☐
6. I believe that if it wasn't for a woman's influence, men would still be living in caves.	☐	☐
7. Behind every successful man there's a loyal woman.	☐	☐
8. If Gloria Steinem is so smart, why isn't she married?	☐	☐
9. No marital argument is so serious it can't be solved with a piece of good jewelry.	☐	☐
10. I love to hear my man's favorite stories over and over again. They get better with each telling.	☐	☐

Scoring:
If most of your answers were "True," it looks like you'll be blissfully happy with a Great Dane. Just keep smiling, check that mirror frequently to make sure your makeup is always fresh, and never let your slip show.

Clothes Make the Man

Your Great Dane will insist on wearing a tie
even for the most casual of occasions.

CHAPTER 10

You and Your
St. Bernard

"UH I'M SORRY HONEY. IS IT THE WRONG COLOR?"

Your St. Bernard is the salt of the earth, so good you sometimes take him for granted. You're probably not dying to show him off to your friends, but although he may not be the most handsome man around, there's none more affectionate and loyal.

The single St. Bernard is a fish out of water. He needs a woman in his life. Even more than sex, he needs a home and family. If you can provide these, you'll have his unflagging devotion for life.

The St. Bernard loves children, and as a father he'll be a pillar of the Little League and the Cub Scouts. Even as a bachelor he's the favorite uncle and the single mother's best friend. But his affection is not limited to children. This is the guy who will find your friend's brother a lawyer and help the local volunteer fire department raise money for a new pumper.

Unfortunately, his warmth and goodness will sometimes lead him to overextend himself. When this happens, his love life (and yours) will suffer. Watch your St. Bernard carefully to be sure he doesn't give too much away.

The Seduceable St. Bernard

Sadly, your saintly St. Bernard's affectionate and generous nature makes him easily seduceable. Your newly-single neighbor or the unhappily married girl at the office are particularly lethal. The neighbor will start by asking his help

fixing leaky faucets or flat tires, and soon escalate into late-night phone calls because she is "afraid." You're the one who should be afraid; this woman is dangerous. The same thing goes for his co-worker. She will start by crying on his shoulder and will soon be sharing intimate conversations with him in a nearby cocktail lounge.

Straying is especially serious when it involves a St. Bernard, because he may be the last man in America who thinks that just because he slept with a woman he owes her something. It's easy for an experienced woman to play on his guilt. From there it's an easy step to "doing the right thing," and the next thing you know he'll be dumping you and marrying her.

Always remember that you are your man's best friend, and it is your *responsibility* to protect him from these predators. Don't advertise his talents to your friends and neighbors. Although his ability as a lover may please you, mentioning it to others will only arouse their curiosity.

The co-workers are a more vexing problem. You must never, under any circumstances, give your St. Bernard the impression that you don't trust him, or worse, don't have confidence in his judgment. Don't criticize the alley cat who's cozying up to him, but subtly point out problems in a constructive manner. Mention that although you know Tiffany is not a tart, it's too bad she dresses like one. Or that it puzzles you that, if Tiffany is as sweet a girl as he says, she has no women friends to confide in. Encourage *him* to encourage *Tiffany* to get a "fresh start" somewhere else—far away from him.

Training Your St. Bernard for Concentration

Do not smile and accept the last-minute calls that take your St. Bernard away from you. Let him know that no-shows and date-lateness, no matter how urgent the reason that called him away, are not acceptable.

Your well-meaning St. Bernard has to learn that his time with you comes first. Sit down with him and block out time that belongs to the two of you. Let him take the lead in this, but be realistic. If he's committed to coaching Little League this spring, don't demand that he see you every weekend in May; settle for weekday nights. If he has a secretary, make sure that he/she knows that this time is reserved.

When you share this special time, make sure it *is* special. That might even mean a quiet evening at home together, in which case, disconnect the phone. And, if you have children, send them to the neighbor's. Soon your St. Bernard will look forward to these private hours. His tail will start wagging at the very thought.

Where to Find a St. Bernard

The St. Bernard is an all-American boy and can be found in your all-American cities. That includes New York (Brooklyn, Queens, and Staten Island, that is), Kansas City, Cleveland, Milwaukee, and Seattle. You'll also find him at Knights of Columbus meetings, union halls, Boy Scout camps, and Ford and Chevrolet auto showrooms. Or just follow the scent of the barbecue grill.

Famous St. Bernards

Alan Alda
Paul Newman
Charles Kuralt
Lavar Burton
Bobby Ewing
Santa Claus
Tom Selleck
Bryant Gumbel
Robert Redford
Ed Asner

Can You Find Happiness with a St. Bernard?

	True	False
1. I think every woman is entitled to breakfast in bed, *especially* if she's a mother.	☐	☐
2. I brake for animals.	☐	☐
3. No holiday seems complete without the children.	☐	☐
4. I like nothing better than a big family barbecue.	☐	☐
5. When I cook I always make enough for company.	☐	☐
6. Why shouldn't I like my boyfriend's mother? She made him what he is.	☐	☐
7. I don't care if my friends think my man is funny-looking.	☐	☐
8. I never met Neil Simon, but he writes as though he lived with us.	☐	☐
9. My home and family are more important to me than my career.	☐	☐
10. I think it's important to help others.	☐	☐

Scoring
If most of your answers were "True," you'll be happy with a St. Bernard. Just be sure you don't end up sharing him with the rest of the world.

Clothes Make the Man

It will take some effort on your part to convince the St. Bernard that he needs to wear a tuxedo when he walks you down the aisle.

CHAPTER 11

You and Your Basset Hound

LET'S
EAT IN
TONIGHT!"

Most people don't notice the Basset Hound, and when he's gone they seldom miss him. With his short, stocky legs and sad and droopy expression, he simply doesn't leave much of an impression. He's not the most exciting guy in the world and not the most successful, but he remains blissfully unaware of all that.

In his off-hours he favors T-shirts with happy faces on them. This is the man who's seen *Porky II* five times and who howls with laughter at the Three Stooges.

Your Basset Hound is known for his easygoing temperament and his great endurance. You'll never train him to be Cary Grant, but if you're not getting any younger, you might consider that he'd make a good husband if not a very exciting one.

Where to Find a Basset Hound of Your Own

- Any McDonald's or Burger King
- Subway token booths
- Behind the counters of large, urban post offices
- Toll booths
- Newsstands (he's selling papers, not buying them)
- TV and appliance repair shops
- Call Xerox and have them send a repairman
- Home video game showrooms
- Your local hardware store (this is a pure nuts and bolts guy)
- Behind the wheel of a UPS truck

Stimulation Training

Because the greatest hazard in a relationship with a Basset Hound is terminal boredom, it's important to begin stimulation training immediately.

He *can* be trained to be less boring and his taste *can* be upgraded. Enroll him in a book club. Encourage him to watch public TV (you might begin with a fund-raising marathon). Give him a subscription to any magazine (except *Mad*) for his birthday. Try to expand his dining horizons by introducing a few "exotic" foods—such as chop suey, spaghetti, and French toast.

Famous Basset Hounds

Don Knotts
Harvey Korman
Murray Greschler

A Word About False Basset Hounds

Jerry Lewis (a Wolf)
Woody Allen (a Wolf)
Jim Nabors (a Poodle)

Can You Find Happiness with a Basset Hound?

	True	False
1. I am 50 years old and I want to have a baby.	☐	☐
2. I am an illegal alien and want to stay in this country.	☐	☐
3. I am 8 months pregnant and want my child to have a father.	☐	☐
4. I have been unemployed for more than one year and need major dental work.	☐	☐
6. I can laugh at anything.	☐	☐
7. No meal is complete without a jellied salad.	☐	☐
8. I think we can all learn something from the Smurfs.	☐	☐
9. I never buy anything that can't be washed in the machine.	☐	☐
10. I can make love to a man who is wearing a lampshade on his head.	☐	☐

Scoring:
If most of your answers were "True," you can find happiness with a Basset Hound. Or maybe all you need is a good rest.

Clothes Make the Man

| Why would any woman find the Basset Hound an agreeable mate? | Surprisingly, even the Basset Hound becomes desirable when properly attired. |

CHAPTER 12

Puppy Love

YOUR PUPPY DISCOVERS 60's MUSIC

"SO HOW MANY GUYS WERE IN THE DAVE CLARK 5?"

Puppies are very cute. They have paws too big for their bodies, wet noses, wonderful, adoring brown eyes, and they wag their little tails incessantly. Walk one in the street and strangers come right up to you and pet them. Everyone, even the most hard-hearted, loves puppies.

It's no wonder, then, that so many women bring home a puppy when they could have chosen a grown man. By a puppy, naturally, I mean any fellow ten or more years younger than you who has not yet had time to develop the characteristics or bad habits of his breed.

Some Well-Known Practitioners of Puppy Love

Britt Eckland
Victoria Principal
Brigitte Bardot
Princess Margaret
Ursula Andress
Sue Ellen Ewing

A Few Advantages of Puppy Love

1. A puppy usually regards his mistress with great awe. It is wonderful to be looked up to that way.
2. Puppies have beautiful, smooth skin (except for those little bumps on face or back) and firm, young, supple muscles.
3. Puppies have enormous energy. They rarely have to take a nap, smoke a cigarette, or wait until the next morning before making love to you again.
4. Puppies tend to be well-informed about the latest pop music; they keep your knowledge of this area up-to-date.
5. Puppies are very appreciative of any little thing you do for them . . . like pay for dinner.
6. Puppies read poetry. If you say, "I measure out my life in coffee spoons," they enthusiastically quote the source . . .

Some Disadvantages of Puppy Love

1. Inviting your puppy to Thanksgiving dinner at your mom's or to office parties may prove a little awkward.
2. Not every woman enjoys explaining what a stretch mark is.
3. Young men tend to meet many nubile and attractive young women; it can make one feel insecure.
4. Your friends will gossip and disapprove (although in fact they may be jealous).
5. Your gay friends will insist upon referring to your puppy as "a trick."

Training Your Puppy to Stay

Puppies seem to fall in love quite easily. If your puppy is young enough, you may be his first love— a position that makes you even more exalted, in his eyes, than his mother. In fact, subliminally, he may come to believe that you *are* his mother.

Your puppy will stay with you as long as you'd like. Naturally, you must continue to share his enthusiasm for the important things in his life: his studies, his relationship with his parents, final exams, computers, choosing a career, and psychedelic drugs.

Marriage

Only a very rich woman can reasonably contemplate marriage to a puppy. Your charms, though they may be intact at the moment, are bound to fade—and plastic surgery, properly done, can be very expensive. Also, as the difference in your ages becomes more and more marked, your puppy will require proportionately more expensive gifts and trinkets (at this juncture, sports cars and motorboats become appropriate gifts). Inevitably, you will have to cope with infidelity. Your puppy may always love you, but given enough time, he'll stray . . .

Where to Find a Puppy of Your Own

1. An Amtrak train to or from Vermont. (He is either on his way to or coming home from boarding school or college.)
2. Punk rock clubs.
3. Scout jamborees.
4. Almost any college campus.
5. Bars near any military base (Camp LeJeune, North Carolina, for example, if your taste runs to young Marines).
6. Your local supermarket (he's the box-boy).
7. Day camps.
8. Pediatric wards.

Ineligible Puppies

1. Your best friend's son; it's too awkward.
2. The mailroom boy. (He will gossip.)
3. Any young man who hangs out on street corners in tight pants in neighborhoods where porn films are being screened.
4. Your nephew or younger cousin.
5. Your own son.

Famous Puppies

Christopher Atkins
Matt Dillon
Tom Cruise
Gary Coleman

If you're *very* wealthy, you might enjoy being married to a puppy.

Can You Find Happiness with a Puppy?

	True	False
1. I'm fascinated with high school and college life and never get tired of hearing about it.	☐	☐
2. I can take the wisdom of Yoda seriously.	☐	☐
3. I'd rather dance than talk anytime.	☐	☐
4. I could watch MTV for hours—it's so stimulating.	☐	☐
5. My body is in such great shape, I don't mind taking my clothes off in front of a much younger man.	☐	☐
6. I wouldn't mind telling my friends his real age.	☐	☐
7. I wouldn't mind telling him *my* real age.	☐	☐
8. I think acne is cute.	☐	☐
9. I've always wanted to attend a prom.	☐	☐
10. I don't mind explaining who Joe Namath, Troy Donohue, and Ed Sullivan were.	☐	☐

Scoring:
If you answered "True" to most of the above, you just might be happiest with a puppy of your own. Just insist that he gets his homework finished before going to bed.

Thumbs up to Puppy love!

CHAPTER 13

What a Good Dog! The Language of Love

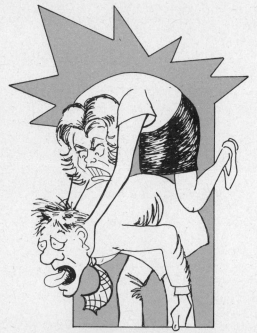

SOMETIMES ACTION SPEAKS LOUDER THAN WORDS.

In my many years of training dogs, I have found that there are certain key words to which dogs respond with great enthusiasm and gusto. For example, after almost any appropriate behavior, I will always say, "What a good dog!" Not, notice, "You good dog!" or "Good dog!" For some reason, dogs respond particularly well to the word "what"—said, of course, with emphasis on the "t." "What a goood dog!" Notice, too, that I pull out the "o's" in good.

Similarly, *men* respond (and do not respond) to certain key words or phrases.

Words to Which Men Respond

huge	(pronounced huuuge; always draw out the "u.") As in "I didn't think it could get so huuuge!"
strong	(pronounced stroong; draw out the "o" slightly.) As in "Strong muscles!" Men are *very* vain about their muscles.
sexy	Every man wants to be sexy.
hot	Every man wants to be hot.
clever	(pronounced cleever; draw out those "e's.") Every man wants you to think he's clever.
wonderful	(pronounced woonderful; the more you draw out those "o's," the more wonderful he is.) As in "That was wonderful!" or "You are such a wonderful lover."
funny	One "u" is sufficient; just make sure that you use it properly: "You are *so* funny!," not "You look funny in those Bermuda shorts . . ."
yes	Every man's favorite word. Except when he's asking if you have been unfaithful, have ever wanted another man, or have ever had a better orgasm.
darling	(pronounced daarliing; draw out both those vowels.) This is a very suitable alternative to "walkies"! Said properly, any decent man will heel to its tune . . .
gift	As in "I have a gift for you," not "Why don't you ever buy me a gift?"
gifted	Most appreciated when you say, "Oh, you are *such* a gifted lover . . ."
massage	(pronounced massaage,) As in "Why don't I give you a nice massage?"
fantastic	(pronounced fantaastic.) As in "You are fantastic!" Almost any context will do, but men are *most* responsive if you use this word in the phrase "That was fantastic!" referring, of course, to their sexual performance.

Phrases to Which Men Respond

Career Phrases:
"You work too hard."
"Why don't you call in sick?"
"Just *let* your boss fire you."
"I'm *glad* you were fired."
"I'll just get a second job."

Sex Phrases:
"What a great kisser."

"I don't like foreplay anyhow."

"Oh, wow! Look at the size of that."
"It feels like the earth's moving."

"I don't think I could take any more pleasure tonight."

Housekeeping Phrases
"How about a nice steak?"

"You just sit there while I clean up."
"Thanks for handing me the mop."
"You're taking out the garbage? How sweet."

Courtship Phrases:
"Let's not tell each other our names."
"My place or yours?"

Phrases to Which Men Do Not Respond

Career Phrases:
"Why don't you work harder?"
"You're calling in sick?"
"Your boss is going to fire you."
"You were *what*?"
"I'll be *damned* if I'm going to work."

Sex Phrases:
"Who taught you how to kiss? Your dog?"
"God gave you a pair of hands and a tongue so you could *use* them."
"No wonder you have such a high voice."
"It feels like something little is inside me."
"My turn."

Housekeeping Phrases
"How about taking me out tonight?"
"You better not just sit there."

"Here's the mop."

"You're taking out the garbage? How apt."

Courtship Phrases:
"Let's get things straight from the beginning."
"The symphony or the ballet?"

"Let's go to my penthouse and you can meet my dog—she's a poodle."

"Let's go to my mother's house and you can meet my father—he's a policeman."

"I have ten erotic zones."

"I have ten children."

"I broke up with my last boyfriend because he was impotent."

"I broke up with my last boyfriend because he was cheap."

"You look *terrific*."

"You're not *seriously* thinking of wearing that, are you?"

"Sometimes I feel guilty about being so rich."

"Sometimes I wonder how I'm going to pay my rent."

"Let's take things slowly—no strings attached."

"When we have children, what do you want to name them?"

"I'm a Playboy bunny."

"I'm a nun."

Words to Which Men Don't Respond

sleep   As in "I don't want you to sleep with other women."

diet   As in "I'm on a diet," or "You need to go on a diet."

don't   Acceptable only when you say "Don't stop . . ."

pregnant   Expect an enthusiastic response only if you are married, and this is a planned pregnancy.

anxious   No man, with the exception of your psychiatrist, wants to hear about your anxiety.

hurry   Acceptable only when you say, "Don't worry, darling, there's no hurry."

What They Say Is Not What They Mean

Men seem to have a cryptic language all their own. In order to as-sist you in figuring out what your man *really* means, with the help of my dear husband, Hercules, I have compiled the following translation guide:

"SURE YOU COULD LOSE FIVE POUNDS. BUT YOU STILL LOOK GREAT IN THAT BIKINI!"

When a Man Says This . . .	He Really Means . . .
Why are you always on the phone with your girlfriends?	Pay more attention to me.
Why do you put up with me?	I'm a helluva great guy, aren't I?
I think I'll stay in town at the Princeton Club one night a week so I can get more work done at the office.	I'm having an affair.
Was that good for you, too?	God, I'm great in bed.
Did you come?	Say yes.
Are you ready to come?	I'm about to come, whether you're ready or not.

Do we have to go to your cousin Jon's?	Your cousin Jon makes me feel inadequate because he makes so much more money than I do.
You have the best body at the party.	It'd be great if your face matched . . .
You always pick friends who aren't as good-looking as you are.	I want to be surrounded by beautiful women. Everybody'll think I'm a great lover.
Those fags are always flirting with me.	I'm having homosexual conflicts.
I want a woman who can cook, clean, and who's read Proust.	Give me a blonde with a great body . . .
I'll never leave you . . .	Not until I get bored . . .
Oh, don't bother making anything special.	The more special, the better.
Money isn't important to me.	I don't have a dime to my name. I hope you still like me.
I think I'm falling in love with you.	Tell me that you love me. Then I'll tell you I decided I'm not falling in love after all.
I don't care what kind of car I drive.	I wouldn't mind a Porsche or a Mercedes, but I can't afford one.
She means nothing to me.	Except hot sex.
I'm not ready to get married.	To you.
I've never even *looked* at another woman.	I'm lying.
Wait until the morning . . .	If you're lucky . . .
This is a great watch (pointing to a picture in a magazine).	Why don't you buy one for me?
I don't know if I can afford you . . .	I'm cheap.
Can't you ever clean up around here?	I want a woman who can cook, clean, has read Proust, and has a great body.

Oh, it was no one . . .

Just my old lover calling to see if we can meet soon. I'm thinking about it . . .

Oh, I don't mind a little extra flesh.

As long as the lights are out.

Her father owns this huge business . . .

Too bad *your* father doesn't have more money . . .

But I'm *always* late!

I refuse to be accountable for my own passive-aggressive behavior.

My father *always* had something on the side.

And so will I.

Can't you ever do anything right?

I'm in such a bad mood you better keep out of my way.

Isn't there anything sweet in the house?

Didn't you bake for me? My mother always made tollhouse cookies.

I'd like to go away for a weekend by myself . . .

I never did tell Susan from Levittown that I was involved with you. She and I would like to go away for a weekend together.

I'm not going to lie to you . . .

. . . I'm going to hurt you instead.

I did *not* say that!

Of course I did! I just won't admit it.

So what if she's attractive?

So what if I slept with her?

That cat is a moron. Why don't you get rid of him?

I don't want you loving anything or anyone but me.

I wouldn't lie to you . . .

Except if it'd save my skin . . .

You're crazy . . .

How dare you remember exactly what I said!

This is the first time I've had a monogamous relationship.

Better enjoy it while it lasts . . .

Do you want to hear the truth?

Why do you make me lie all the time?

I'm no good . . .

Please love me anyway. But I'm telling you the truth; I'm no good.

Pet Names

Pet names are those special diminutives or terms of endearment that express a couple's affinity and bond. Sometimes, as with Lady Bird or Jackie, these private names become public, catch on, and are the names by which a person is known by all. Pet names can be very charming.

Naturally, a true Lovehouse Woman will recognize that certain pet names for the man in her life are more appropriate than others.

Acceptable Pet Names	*Unacceptable Pet Names*
Darling	Rover
Dr. Delight	Spot
Honey	Old Yeller
Sexy	Fang
You Big Thing	Tiny

CHAPTER 14

Some Rewarding Tricks to Teach Your Man

A trick is any special little action that brings pleasure to both of you. Although it doesn't come naturally, a well-trained man will pick it up in no time. That's one of the wonderful things about men: their *malleability*. If you go about it correctly, you can get them to do just about whatever you'd like. A true Lovehouse Woman, of course, will never abuse this privilege. But just in case some of your training skills are rusty, here are some invaluable tips from the Lovehouse School.

Complimenting Your Body OR "Only Smart Men Think I'm Pretty"

Stand in front of him in your sexiest underwear. Look half in a nearby mirror and half at him. Say, "Don't I look fabulous today?"

When he nods his head, say, "Gee, I wish you'd tell me that more often." (*Note:* If he doesn't nod his head, roll up a newspaper, hold it over the part of his body he values the most, and ask your question again.)

The Flowers Trick OR "Say It with Flowers or Else"

You have already said that you *love* flowers, but he hasn't responded. Next time you go out to dinner, note his MasterCard number. Use it to call in an order at your favorite florist. Have the florist enclose a card that reads "You deserve these." Show the flowers *and* the card to your man. Insist that you *know* your man sent them. Do this every single day. With luck, he will get the hint before the bill.

"WOULDN'T IT BE FUN TO MAKE LOVE ON THIS?"

Fur Coat Tricks OR "Wouldn't It Be Fun to Make Love on This?"

It's true: He's rich and you're cold. Unfortunately, those facts alone are not going to get you anything more than a hot water bottle. If you want

fur, you can't fight fair. One of the best ways to secure a fur coat is to catch your man in bed with his boss's wife. But if blackmail isn't your cup of tea, consider the following:

Next time your man is in an especially good mood (he received a promotion or made a big sale) take him for a walk in a shopping mall or a major department store with a good fur salon. Suggest going in "just to look." Model a few coats for him. Try to use these helpful phrases as you do:

"Fur coats make me feel so sexy."
"There's something about fur that makes me feel like a tiger."
"Wouldn't it be fun to make love on this?"
"I wonder what it would feel like to wear this and nothing else?"

If he hasn't offered to buy your fur by this time, all is not lost. When the salesperson asks if you'll take it, kiss your man, hug him, and thank him profusely. Tell him how wonderful he is, and let him decide if it will be cash or charge while you carry the fur out to your car.

Marriage Tricks OR "Surprise! It's a Wedding!"

Even though he enjoyed being introduced to you last week, marriage may strike your man as a frightening and awesome step. For that very reason, it's up to you to conquer his fears and get him to take the plunge. Let me give you some alternatives and you can choose the one that works for you.

1. *Pretend you're pregnant.* Although this once-popular method has declined in popularity in recent years, it can still be effective under the proper circumstances. I suggest showing up at his mother's house with a pillow under your blouse and a gun pointed at your head. Remind his mother how messy brains would look on her white shag carpet. Have a justice of the peace waiting outside the door.

2. *Call his best friend and suggest that a bachelor party is in order.* This trick works best if his best friend is a practical joker or an idiot.

3. *Get another offer.* Tell your man that you have decided to marry someone else, even if you have to make up some beau. Make it clear that you are very *fond* of this new rival, but fonder of course of your man. That should get him moving. This technique is especially effective with the Great Dane, who is usually slow to move (he has to think everything over very carefully), but who will move very swiftly indeed when faced with some competition. It's also effective with the Wolf, but why would you want *him*?

4. *Tell him you have a terminal illness and your only wish is to be married before you die.* (You may have to assure him that your health insurance will cover your bills, but that's just his practical side showing.) Next year, you can tell him that his love has caused a miracle— you're cured!

5. *Get him drunk.* Next day, ask him when he wants to set the date, and insist he asked you to marry him.

6. *Tell him you have been born*

again and can't sleep with him anymore. Amazing, but true, men will get married just to have sex.

Give him a surprise wedding at your local church or synagogue. Invite all his friends and *relatives.* Everyone loves a surprise and what could be more exciting than a surprise wedding? Imagine the look on his face when he hears the organ boom out "Here Comes the Bride."

"THIS IS A STRANGE PLACE TO HOLD A COSTUME PARTY."

CHAPTER 15

Curing Your Man's Fears

Sometimes, we don't get to choose our dogs: They choose us. They wander into the backyard, scratch at the door, and look up with those beguiling eyes. Almost before you know it, you've adopted a new pet and someone else's problems are now yours.

Adoption isn't always easy. Some pets have been abused, some have been spoiled. *Most* strays do seem to carry a few scars . . .

Like dogs, men arrive on our doorsteps with an unknown past. Your man, no doubt, has had a jarring emotional experience in his past that has left him terrified. This fear or phobia may be triggered by words such as "diet" or "marriage" or by the smell of a barbershop. Some men even cringe at the sight of large bodies of water. Some women learn to live with these phobias, stretching and bending their own needs to accommodate their men. I say this is totally unnecessary: Your man can be trained out of any fear.

Fear of Ties

This is one of the most common phobias around and one of the most dangerous. If tolerated early in the relationship, this will escalate into fear of suits, as in "No, I won't go to your friend Sabrina's wedding because I'd have to wear a suit," and eventually you'll find your choice of restaurants limited to those that don't require a jacket and tie. Extreme cases have refused promotions on the grounds that it would mean a change of dress. I'm sure you understand therefore why such a phobia must be dealt with immediately.

Ironically enough, most men seldom connect their way of dressing with yours. A man in a T-shirt and jeans would be perfectly comfortable beside a woman in a silk dress, stockings, and the highest of heels. In fact, he'd prefer it.

Treatment

Treat your man to dinner in the best restaurant in town. Let him know ahead of time that a jacket and tie are required. Viewing this as a special treat, he will of course eagerly don the jacket and tie. Praise him and tell him how good he looks.

When you arrive at the restaurant, observe out loud that the

THE FAY WRAY
SYNDROME:

YOU WEAR A GOWN
AND HEELS AND HE
COMES AS IS.

maitre d' seems to think he is a celebrity.

During dinner, stroke him frequently on the upper sleeve and tell him again how good he looks. You might even suggest skipping dessert and having the waiter wrap it up for you to take home.

As I describe this to you, I can't help recalling the first time I tried this technique with my darling husband at the Bakery Restaurant outside Chicago. The evening went so well that later that night I let him bind my wrists with his yellow silk tie while we made love. I don't mind telling you that I've had a hard time getting him into casual clothes ever since.

Fear of Haircuts

This is a good example of a childhood phobia, that if not dealt with immediately, will hang on well into the adult years. For the small boy, the haircut is traumatic because in his childish mind he assumes that the hair is part of him, and cutting it will hurt. In adolescence it becomes a symbol of control. The teenage boy controls very little in his life, but he can control his haircuts, if only by delaying them.

Treatment

Get him an appointment with the best barber in town. (This can be offered to him as a present.) Then "forget" about the appointment (except to be sure that he keeps it).

When you see him that night, don't mention the haircut. Instead, ask him what he's been up to all day, because he looks so good. Leave it to him to realize that it's his new haircut that makes the difference. Leave it to the barber to tell him that he should come in every two weeks.

Fear of Shaving

It's quite possible that one of the most heartbreaking revelations after marriage is the discovery that your man, so carefully groomed and clean shaven in the outside world, likes to pass up the razor on his days off. Or, to put it another way, *you don't count.* This is the beginning of being taken for granted and must absolutely be nipped in the bud. A "No shave, no kiss" rule must be initiated and strictly enforced. When Max starts to nuzzle your cheek with that wire brush of his, he must be halted at once and told that he's hurting you.

Treatment

Now, a man may truly have some good reasons for not shaving. Do not ask him what they are. Do not discuss them! You'll only be distracted. Instead, I suggest allowing him to sleep on Saturday morning. While he is snoozing, gently paint an amusing design on his face with Mercurochrome or iodine. Be creative. Best is writing "Shave Me" on both cheeks. He'll get the message.

Fear of Soap and Water

If grown dogs are just big puppies, most men are just tall boys and must be dealt with as such. Too many men think that a day off from work is a holiday from grooming. You can train your man to keep clean by emphasizing that on work days he's grooming for others, but on the weekend he's grooming for you.

Treatment

Make this your most sensual time together. Share a shower. Take turns washing each other's hair. Volunteer to give him a shave, Japanese geisha style.

Always remember that a healthy, happy man has sleek, shiny skin, squeaky clean hair, and smooth close-shaven cheeks.

Fear of Intimacy

Another quirk unique to the male species and with the potential to be the most tragic of all—if not for him, for you. Learn to recognize and acknowledge these signs:

1. He resists meeting your family, offering excuses like, "I have to have my car washed that day."
2. He resists meeting your friends, and having met them, struggles to avoid exposure to them again.
3. He limits the time you spend together to weekends only, or weeknights only; limited periods that he can control.
4. Although genuinely sensitive, kind, and loving in private, he puts you down in front of others.
5. He resists any display of affection not related directly to sex.

Treatment

The man who fears intimacy is the most phobic man around and must be treated with the utmost delicacy. It will be a long time before he can be exposed to double dating, group trips to Disney World, and Thanksgiving dinner with your mom and dad.

Begin by recognizing that you must never, never turn down an invitation because he is unable or unwilling to go. Instead, select someone else, anyone but a Poodle, but preferably a man of his own breed. *Nothing* makes a Wolf more wary than the presence of another Wolf, and it's a fact that the Great

Dane simply cannot take any other breed seriously. Get photographs of the occasion and share them with him. When he sees how easily he can be replaced by one of the same breed, he'll shape up.

Present an invitation as a business proposition. This works especially well with the Great Dane who, no matter what his emotional weaknesses, will always rise to the success bait. Equating worldly success with manliness, he couldn't possibly pass up a chance to better himself.

Gradually introduce him to shared activities, but keep them casual. "Accidentally" meet friends on line at the movies. If he seems comfortable talking with them, move on to coffee at a diner nearby.

Fear of Marriage

Frankly, I find this fear not half so daunting as fear of intimacy. Too many women think that marriage will cure fear of intimacy, and it won't. Both fears must be dealt with separately.

Treatment

Do not, above all, try to lull him or yourself into a false sense of security by moving in together. A Living Together Arrangement is *not* a marriage.

Instead, begin by gently exposing him to happily married couples. Suggest spending Sundays in an amusement park, where you're likely to see happy families.

In truly severe cases, I recom-
mend drastic action. See Marriage Tricks (page 67–8).

Neurotic Behaviors

Hitting

A man hits for several reasons. You may think a hitter hits because he is upset. But you are wrong. He hits because he wants to be the master. In sensible circles this is simply *not* allowed. Another reason: Someone thought it was cute when he did it at five.

In some ways, a mother's advice may be a lot smarter than it sounds at the time. When I was a young woman, my own dear mum gave me some advice that I will pass on to you: If a man *ever* hits you, pick up the nearest frying pan (preferably cast iron) and smash him over the head with it.

There is *no* excuse for *any* woman to tolerate a man who hits.

Chronic Depression

Over the years, I have effectively and perfunctorily dealt with chronic depression in dogs by a few simple jerks on the choke chain. But this does not work with men. In fact, as far as I am aware, *nothing* works with a chronically depressed man, at least not for more than a few hours. As far as I am concerned, and after much prolonged study, I must say that there are only two ways of dealing with a love pet's chronic depression: (1) leave him or (2) electroshock therapy (i.e., a plugged-in toaster or hair dryer thrown into his bathwater).

Neurotic behavior cannot be tolerated.

CHAPTER 16

My Mailbag

For those women who live too far away to bring their men in to be trained, I am always available for consultations by mail. I find that some of my most fascinating cases have been brought to me by my mailman. Let me share a few with you.

Dear Dr. Lovehouse:

I went over to my sister's house the other night, only to find her in the arms of a man who is *not* her husband. Meanwhile, the man who *is* her husband was in the kitchen cooking chicken Kiev for my sister and her "friend." Don't you find this a little sick?

Disgusted in Detroit

Dear Disgusted:

What's wrong with chicken Kiev?

**Love,
Barbara**

Dear Dr. Lovehouse:

Rex, my love, has never been faithful. I thought that if I were patient he'd outgrow his tendency to roam, but he's worse than ever. I know he cares about me, and when he's with me it's like I'm the only woman in the world. Yet when he's away I know he's with someone else. This has been going on for thirteen years and I don't think I can take it anymore.

Sobbing in St. Paul

Dear Sobbing:

Quit your blubbering and get out your checkbook! For only $39.99 your man can be the proud owner of his very own Cheat-No-More-Shorts. These sleek, snakeskin panties contract the moment your man puts them on and . . . PRESTO! . . . he's monogamous. Remember: A constricted man is a *restricted* man when he's wearing his Boa Briefs.

**Love,
Barbara**

Dear Dr. Lovehouse:

Last week my husband asked me to go to the furrier's with him. He had me try on several fur coats, including a sable. I watched him pay for the coat and heard him tell the furrier to deliver it. Barbara, I was *so* excited, and waited home each day so that I wouldn't miss the delivery truck. Yesterday, worrying that the coat hadn't arrived, I went to my husband's office to see what was wrong. When I got off the elevator, who should I see but my husband's secretary wearing *a brand new sable coat.* I asked her where she got it. She said my husband had given it to her. Barbara, my husband has always been faithful to me, always been good and kind. How could he do this to me? What's wrong with him?

Confused in Kincaid

Dear Confused:

There's only one thing wrong with your husband: He's alive.

**Love,
Barbara**

Dear Dr. Lovehouse:

My former boyfriend, Hassan, never took me anywhere. I tried to train him by refusing to see him unless he had a real evening planned, but that only made him stop calling. Now I hear he's dating another woman and taking her to all the nice places he never took me. I don't understand. I'm just as good as she is.

Pining in Peoria

Dear Pining:

Goodness has nothing to do with it. You have simply demonstrated one of the saddest rules of training: It is almost impossible for the same woman to train a man once she's botched up the job. You *trained* him to spend evenings at your place or his, even if you did this unconsciously, and now you can't expect to *retrain* him to take you out. The woman who replaced you may not be as pretty or as smart, but she started him off right. The best you can do now is learn your lesson and apply it to the next man. As for a second chance at this one, wait at least a year until the woman he's now seeing has purged him of your bad habits before you even consider trying again.

**Love,
Barbara**

Dear Dr. Lovehouse:

Clancy comes from a terrible home.
He was very poor and his mom and
dad abused him. Now he's an actor
and out of work a lot. He spends most
of the day drinking with the guys and
then comes home and hits on me. I
know he's depressed and unhappy,
but how can I get him to stop taking
it out on me?

Disappointed in Denver

Dear Disappointed:

**Stop trying to explain this cur's
behavior and recognize that he's
a rogue animal. Normally, we'd
put such a pitiful case to sleep,
but there are laws against this in
most states. Do the next best
thing and bury this relationship
like a tired old bone.**

**Love,
Barbara**

Dear Dr. Lovehouse:

I love to collect Depression glass, patchwork quilts, and old-fashioned dolls. My idea of a great day is to drive into the country and go from antique shop to antique shop, or to visit one of those big outdoor collectibles shows. My boyfriend, Thor, thinks these things are boring. How can I get him to share my interests?

Secondhand in Roseland

Dear Secondhand:

Surely he must agree to go with you once in a while! Next time he does, concentrate on finding something that interests *him*. If he's handy and loves tools, make sure he sees any of the beautiful old woodworking tools. Whatever his interests are, from baseball to politics, there's sure to be something there for him. Whatever it is, if he doesn't buy it for himself, buy it for him as a present. He'll be so pleased that he'll be eager to accompany you on the next outing. *Note:* If all this fails, change your hobby and start collecting rings from Tiffany's . . . on your man's charge account, of course.

**Love,
Barbara**

Dear Dr. Lovehouse:

I think it's despicable to train a man. Men are no better and no worse than women. Personally, I like my man just the way he is.

Happy in Hicksville

Dear Happy:

Oh grow up . . .

Love,
Barbara

Dear Dr. Lovehouse:

I met a man who is intelligent, kind, wealthy, witty, and ugly as all sin. Barbara, I love him dearly when the lights are out, but when the lights are on, I cringe. What to do?

Grossed-Out in Grovers Corners

Dear Grossed-Out:

Sunglasses worked for Jackie O., why not for you?

**Love,
Barbara**

Dear Dr. Lovehouse:

Stephen is the best lover I've had. His only fault is that he doesn't say anything to me while we're in bed. Can you help?

Quiet in Quincy

Dear Quiet:

Make phone calls while having sex.

**Love,
Barbara**

CHAPTER 17

The Ten Most Common Mistakes Women Make with Men

1. Waiting for Home Delivery

Many women continue to believe that one day, without their having to do one single thing, Mr. Right is going to show up on the doorstep. Darlings, I can't emphasize this point enough. When it comes to men, there is no such thing as home delivery!

He is not going to ring your bell one evening, tell you that he's been watching you from afar for the past month and has decided you are the woman of his dreams.

In fact, if such a man should ever appear at your door, call the police *immediately.*

You will have to go out and look for him. Remember, no dog ever wins a prize without entering the show ring.

2. Picking the Wrong Breed

Even if the man you have is not exactly perfect, you can train him to be what you want. But there are limits.

A dear little Basset Hound is never going to turn into a Great Dane. All the training in the world won't make those little legs grow. Conversely, if you really want a Poodle, you're never going to be happy with a St. Bernard. They slobber too much. Pick your breed first . . . and wisely.

3. Trying to Change Him

You saw those beautiful, gleaming white teeth, you loved the way he licked your . . . nose, and suddenly you've found yourself hopelessly enmeshed with a Wolf. You decide that with a little taming, he can become the family pet.

Forget all those illusions about white picket fences. He may seem docile, but to keep this breed fenced in, you're going to have to admit what he is and order extremely strong chain link. *Breeds never change.*

4. Giving More than You Receive

It is *not* more blessed to give than to receive, no matter what your mother told you. This means that the very first time you receive an inexpensive bottle of very ordinary cologne for your birthday after you've dropped $85 at Gucci's for a key case (and they charged you $18 extra for the monogram), you are at the beginning of a long downhill slide.

Take steps.

5. Forgiving Bad Behavior

Bad behavior is not to be forgiven, it is to be *corrected.*

6. Lending Him Money

Never mind his child support and alimony, a lady never discusses money with a man. You should keep your bank balance as deep a secret as that little fling in Marrakesh last year.

If he says he only has five dollars until payday, tell him he's three up on you.

7. Pretending to Be What You're Not

If you see the beach as only a damp place where sand gets into your white wine, and he loves going there, allow him a run once in a while, but don't agree with such alacrity to these tiresome jaunts or you will be drinking gritty white wine for the rest of your life. And that wears your teeth down.

8. Being Too Eager to Get a Commitment

Most men require some time to realize that they adore and need you. You *must* hold back a bit—no matter how sure you are of your own affections—and wait for your fellow to give you a cue. Think of it as a kind of dance of the heart; in this, as in other dances, your man should be under the impression that he always leads.

9. Giving Unclear Signals

Say what you mean and mean what you say. Telepathy with your pet will develop over time. But if you say, "I don't care if you *never* attend another Thanksgiving dinner at my cousin Violet's," your man will think you mean it, and you may never see cousin Violet again.

10. Forgetting to Praise

Your man thrives on praise—especially *your* praise. *Always* praise correct behavior. But, more than that . . . praise the way your man looks, praise his love skills, praise his taste in jewelry (you know you *can* cultivate that), praise how well he handled himself that day at the office or store, praise how well he plays basketball . . . There's always something you can praise him for; the list is practically endless. No man can be praised too much.

CHAPTER 18

Tails Up!

Sexual attraction provides the real axis of the male-female relationship. Without the promise of coital delirium, many women would rather skip men entirely. Yet, miraculous experience that heterosexual pleasure can be at its best, one must *never* allow oneself to be held in thrall by "that thing" or its owner. Remember, ladies, God and Mother Nature did rather well by you, too . . .

Today, we live in a "free" society, with the horrendous pressures that entails: college entrance examinations, cutthroat jockeying for positions of power and wealth, and the freedom to marry whatever floozy one wishes. It's no wonder so many of our men are so beleaguered and not quite as sexy as they could be . . .

Unlike the modern dog, which has had at least 2000 years to evolve from wild beast to tame, lovable, household pet, modern man has had to make the transition much more quickly. The simple truth is that the strain on their nervous systems has been acute, because it did not have time to evolve sufficiently to cope with rush-hour traffic, mortgage payments, private

school and college tuition bills, and wives and girlfriends who express political opinions and work as interior decorators.

As I see it, it is therefore modern woman's duty to soothe her man to the point where he can more easily achieve "tails up" position: Nervous men do *not* make good lovers.

Men, for example, love physical contact. Try massaging his back in a circular motion, repeating in a low, warm voice, "What a strong back." Occasionally, kiss his back. You must be the judge as to how passionate these kisses should be. Some men enjoy a few bruises. This is especially true of professional athletes who spend a lot of time undressed in the locker room. Others, including squash and rugby players, are less comfortable showing off "love bites."

Another tried-and-true Lovehouse calmer-downer is (believe it or not) a nice, hot, fragrant bubble bath. Naturally, he sits in the tub and you give it to him. Make sure, of course, that the water is not *too* hot, as you don't want the man of your dreams to have a heart attack. Make sure, too, that the scent you use is something manly like musk-scented bubble bath, or mix your own: three or four caps of Canoe or Vetiver, for example, added to a nice, neutral-scented shampoo, squeezed into the filling tub. Again, using a nice, soft washcloth in a gentle, circular motion, repeat in a low, warm voice, "What magnificent muscles you have"; "How beautiful your chest hair looks, wet like this"; or "Look at that big cock float."

Take extra pains with his feet. Massage them soundly. Pull the toes ever so slightly. Do not neglect the metatarsal. Be sure to rub the arch where it gets so very tired.

Soft music in the background always helps. Candlelight would be superb. Naturally, if you have a pretty figure, it would be appropriate to perform these ablutions attired in skimpy, suggestive underwear, or a cute little chemise or "teddy." When he emerges from the tub, of course you dry him off.

But massage is not everything . . . Another wonderful mid-winter or chilly autumn evening calmer is a nice hot bowl of homemade soup.

My own Hercules does love his beef soup with vegetables and barley, or a good hot plate of Ukranian borscht. These soups are so easy to make; they freeze well and they most definitely work: I can attest to that.

Another nice calmer is what I call the Midnight Stroke. Properly done, your man will never know it's gone on; he'll just wake up calmer, happier, at peace with you and the world. This is a very natural extension of a daytime or evening massage.

Simply wait until your dear pet has fallen off into slumberland, then gently, ever so gently, rub his back, especially the lower back, and those gorgeous buttocks. Remember, this is just a nice, soft, gentle massage; you do not want to wake your Sleeping Prince. Periodically during the night, as your man sleeps, rouse yourself enough to perform this simple but devoted service for him.

Naturally, as calm as this will make him, he'll wake "tails up" to you—and a nice, fresh day . . .

CHAPTER 19

Test Your Training Skills

Now is a good time to test your training skills. I have two tests, one for single women and one for those of you who are married. (Dr. Lovehouse does not believe in living together and considers it evidence of temporary insanity.) Let's start with the singles.

Obedience School

A Test for Singles

1. **Your handsome ex-boyfriend Andrew is having a lavish wedding and you must have a date. Corky, the man you have been dating for four months, suddenly refuses to attend the wedding with you. You decide to:**
   (a) Go alone, look fantastic, and have a wonderful time.
   (b) Go with Andrew. Why should the groom lack a date?
   (c) Go alone, tell everyone Corky is in the hospital, and say you promised to bring back a floral centerpiece for him.
   (d) Bring a Poodle as your date and spend the whole time listening to him ridicule the gowns, makeup, food, and band.

2. **It's your first date and Butch shows up with a bottle of Ripple and a copy of a TV guide. You**
   (a) Smile and say, "How thoughtful, now we can really get to know each other."
   (b) Tear the TV guide to bits and tell him you'd only use that wine to set your hair.

(c) Say, "How thoughtful; my drain was clogged." Immediately pour the wine into your kitchen sink. Then ask why he brought the TV guide. When he tells you, laugh and compliment his sense of humor.

(d) Scream, "Is this your idea of a date?"

3. **Marco is very suave. You know you're not the only woman he's seeing, so how do you get him to concentrate his full attention on you?**

(a) Call every woman in his address book, say you're from the Department of Health, and gravely explain that Marco has a highly contagious, loathsome venereal disease; advise them to have a test immediately.

(b) Recognize that Marco is a Wolf and start seeing other men.

(c) Remember the words of Lady Bird Johnson and "try to discover the special qualities that attracted him" to the other women.

(d) Be so charming, so supportive, so attentive, and so *nice* that he has no choice but to spend more time with you.

4. **When you met Dom you were attracted to his support of women's liberation, but on your second date he suggested splitting the cost of two 7-Ups. You**

(a) Thank your lucky stars that you have found a man who practices what he preaches and who treats you as an equal partner, because you believe this is the basis for a sharing relationship.

(b) Hit him gently on the nose with a rolled-up newspaper and send him back to his kennel.

(c) Pull out your own wallet and pay your half of the bill.

(d) Touch his thigh, look him sincerely in the eye, and say, "Is it true cheap men are impotent?" Don't bother to find out.

Answers:

1. (a) and (b) are both correct.
   (c) is acceptable only if the centerpiece is poison ivy.
   (d) will only make Corky happy.

2. (a) is satisfactory only if he's a Basset Hound you don't want to be seen with.

(b) and (c) are both correct.

(d) is to be used only with a Wolf—you can never have him defensive enough.

3. (b) is correct, although (a) is certainly worth trying.

(c) and (d) are pathetic.

4. (d) is correct, although (b) is acceptable.

(c) proves either you or he is a wimp.

(a) is delusional

Graduate Obedience School

A Test for Marrieds

---

1. **Herbie is a telephonalic. Since you've been married, your long distance bills have skyrocketed. His phone bills are starting to cut into your food budget. You**

(a) Grin and bear it.

(b) Serve Herbie a nice dinner and calmly explain to Herbie that he's wasting money.

(c) Serve Herbie baked phone for dinner; no explanation necessary.

(d) Investigate discount phone services and get the cheapest one you can find.

2. **You have been after Apollo for three weeks to take down the storm windows. You've almost given up reminding him when suddenly he's done it. Now is the time to**

(a) Give him a kiss, but say "It's about time."

(b) Check his work to see if there's anything he missed.

(c) Get on your knees and weep with gratitude.

(d) Kiss him, praise him, and make his favorite dessert three nights in a row.

(e) Call your neighbor in to see what a great job he did.

THE WELL-TRAINED MAN ENJOYS CHANGING DIAPERS.

3. **When you and Ralph married, you didn't expect it to end your dating, but you realize it's been three weeks since you have even gone out to dinner. How can you put the magic back in your relationship?**

    (a) Make plans immediately for a night out, including dinner and a show. Order the tickets for the show with *his* credit card.

    (b) Think of a wonderful place you visited early in your relationship and suggest going back there. Tell him you'll help him cook dinner one night next week if he takes you.

    (c) Speaking to him as a rational adult, state the problem, and ask why he's behaving this way.

    (d) Tell him you're tired of cooking and you want to go out, adding if he expects you to continue living with him, he'll have to accept that.

  (e) Tell him about the wonderful places where Suzie's
      boyfriend takes her.

4. **You come home from work and find that the house is a
    mess and dinner is still in the freezer. You**
  (a) Take your man out to dinner.
  (b) Clean the house and start cooking.
  (c) Throw a tantrum.
  (d) Throw your man out of the house.
  (e) Assume your man has been in some terrible accident and
      call the local hospital. Why *else* would a well-trained man
      leave such a mess?

Answers:

1. (a) and (d) won't cure Herbie of his affliction.
  (b) is for martyrs only.
  (c) is the correct answer.

2. (c) and (d) are for martyrs only.
  (e) will embarrass Apollo if your neighbor is a man and interest
      your neighbor if she is a woman.
  (a) and (b) are correct.

3. (a) and (b) are correct.
  (c) is totally inappropriate. We are not dealing with a rational
      adult; we are dealing with a man.
  (d) Only a Basset Hound will accept an ultimatum and do you
      really want to be seen in public with one?
  (e) Certain techniques may arouse a competitive nature, but this
      isn't one of them.

4. (a) and (b) are for martyrs only.
  (c) will make your voice hoarse.
  (d) will make your back ache.
  (e) is the correct answer.

CHAPTER 20

When to Send Your Man to the Pound

"STILL DON'T THINK I LOOK FABULOUS TODAY?"

Now ladies, you know that the message of this book is that there are *no bad men*. Well . . . I lied. There are *almost* no bad men.

Unfortunately, even after rigorous training, some men retain their bad behavior and must be abandoned.

Fifty Reasons to Leave Your Lover
(At the Pound)

1. He orders anchovies on the pizza.
2. He guesses your weight . . . correctly.
3. After 30 years of putting up with his habitual unemployment, you divorce him. The day after the divorce is final, he wins the lottery.
4. You have been living together for 16 years. He said he'd marry you. He hasn't.
5. He takes a photograph of you without makeup.
6. He *shows* someone the photograph he took of you without makeup.
7. He tells you that your face-lift has aged you.
8. He puts the right number of candles on your birthday cake.
9. You ask him if you remind him of Katharine Hepburn. He says no.
10. He cancels your credit cards.
11. At a dinner party he tells a "funny story" about the time you ate an entire cheesecake at two o'clock in the morning.
12. When someone compliments him on your looks, he laughs and says, "You should see her in the morning. Then you'd *really* be impressed."
13. He changes the channels without asking.
14. He asks if his aging mother can move in.
15. He asks if his aging mother can sleep in your bedroom.
16. He buys you a garbage can on your anniversary.
17. He buys you power tools on your anniversary.
18. He hangs a photograph of Brooke Shields over your bed.
19. He informs you that the daughter from his first marriage who has been living at your house for a year is actually not his daughter.
20. He wakes you to ask if you are asleep.
21. When you get angry with him, he asks you if you're "going through the change."
22. For your birthday, he has each of your seven children give you a baby duck. You live in a high-rise apartment building.
23. He tells you he's too young to get married.
24. He tells you he's too old to get married.

25. He suggests that you would weigh less if you ate less.
26. He asks a group of women if it's true that *everybody* has stretch marks.
27. He turns on the radio when you sing.
28. He buys you a house . . . next door to his mother's.
29. He informs you that he is sick of the rat race and has just quit his executive job in order to do something meaningful with his life: like sleep more.
30. When you show him a picture of yourself taken when you were seventeen, he tells you that you *used to be* a real knockout.
31. On your golden anniversary, you ask if he'd do it all over again. He laughs . . .
32. When you eat at his mother's house, he says, "Oh boy! Vegetables! I haven't had *those* in ages!"
33. He gives you a surprise party. All the guests are women. You don't know any of them.
34. One night when you have both been drinking, he talks you into letting him cut your hair.
35. The day before your wedding, he informs you that he has something to confess. He's gay.
36. He offers to take your clothes to the dry cleaner's. The dry cleaner is closed. He takes your clothes to the laundry instead.
37. Your see your man's photo—at the post office.
38. He goes fishing and brings his catch home—alive.
39. You overhear him tell someone on the phone that he "prefers plain women to pretty women, because plain women are so grateful."
40. You find prophylactics in his coat pocket. You are on the Pill.
41. As the two of you drive past a motel, he points and says, "Remember the great night we spent there?" You don't.
42. He tells you that you remind him of his mother.
43. He tells you that you remind him of *your* mother.
44. He refuses to buy a dishwasher on the grounds that "dishpan hands are sexy." His hands have never touched water in his life.
45. You ask him to tell you his secret sex fantasy. He does.

46. He tells someone what the inside of your purse looks like.
47. When you get a cold, his first question is whether you have life insurance.
48. At weddings, he won't let you try to catch the bouquet.
49. He tells people that you snore.
50. He believes that female orgasm is a myth.

All my men are good men . . . or it's off to the pound with them!